THE WALLS OF

Rudolph Fisher (1897–1934) was born in Washington D.C., the youngest of three children born to Reverend John Wesley Fisher, a Baptist pastor, and Glendora Williamson Fisher. He graduated with honours from Classical High School in Providence, Rhode Island, going on to Brown University and subsequently the illustrious Howard University Medical School, specialising in research into early radiology. Also a writer and musician, Fisher was an active participant in the Harlem Renaissance, the arts revolution that swept New York in the 1920s, and a supporter of Pan-Africanism and the broader struggle for black labour privilege and women's empowerment.

Fisher was said to be 'one of the wittiest writers of his generation', winning acclaim for several short stories including 'High Yaller', which won the literary prize of the black magazine *The Crisis*. In 1928 his first novel, *The Walls of Jericho*, was published to rave reviews. In the previous year Fisher had opened his own practice as a radiographer in New York City, and continued to serve as a superintendent of the International Hospital in Harlem even as *The Conjure-Man Dies*, his second novel, was being hailed as the first African-American detective novel when published in 1932.

As a writer, Fisher was at his most masterful when illustrating the day-to-day reality of ordinary people's lives. While depicting the harsh conditions and racial divisions within the black community, he strived to portray a balanced view of life as he saw it with a touch of humour. Nowhere else in classical black fiction is the tenacity of the average black man and woman in the face of adversity so celebrated. Dr Fisher died in 1934 at the age of 37, seemingly as a result of exposure to his own X-ray machines, and one can only speculate about what he would have achieved had he lived longer.

By the same author

The Conjure-Man Dies

RUDOLPH FISHER

The Walls of Jericho

HarperCollins*Publishers*

HarperCollins*Publishers*
1 London Bridge Street
London SE1 9GF
www.harpercollins.co.uk

HarperCollins*Publishers*
1st Floor, Watermarque Building, Ringsend Road
Dublin 4, Ireland

This paperback edition 2021

1

First published by Alfred A. Knopf, New York 1928
'One Month's Wages' first published in *The City of Refuge (Rev. Ed.)*
by the University of Missouri Press 2008
Preface first published by The X Press 1995
Introduction first published by Arno Press Inc. 1969

Rudolph Fisher asserts his moral right
to be identified as the author of this work

This novel is entirely a work of fiction. It is presented in its original form
and depicts ethnic, racial and sexual prejudices that were commonplace
at the time it was written.

A catalogue record for this book is available from the British Library

ISBN 978-0-00-844435-8

Typeset in Bulmer MT Std by
Palimpsest Book Production Ltd, Falkirk, Stirlingshire
Printed and bound in Great Britain by CPI Group (UK) Ltd,
Croydon CRO 4YY

MIX
Paper from
responsible sources
FSC™ C007454

This book is produced from independently certified FSC™ paper
to ensure responsible forest management.

For more information visit: www.harpercollins.co.uk/green

PREFACE

THE SUCCESSFUL young lawyer Fred Merrit's move onto the highly exclusive Court Avenue would, under any other circumstance, cause no comment. The fact that the dashing, cherubic faced, fair-skinned, blond-haired gentleman in question is in fact black puts a whole new twist on things (to say the least). Not only is he the topic of conversation in the genteel home of Miss Agatha Cramp, his spinster neighbour and her cronies, but also at the foremost male watering-hole, Patmore's. Here the likes of Jinx, Bubber, Shine, Patmore himself and others wonder at the motive of this white Negro—termed 'dickty' in Rudolph Fisher's novel.

In a time when colour is all too often the determining factor of one's status in life, Merrit and Shine are on opposite sides of the social spectrum. In their separate ways they are both content and fulfilled with their respective lots. Merrit has a sound education behind him and a burgeoning legal career ahead and socializes with like-minded individuals. Whilst Shine, the foreman of a small but highly efficient removal team consisting of his best friends, is equally content. He derives his happiness from driving Bess, his beloved removal van, playing cards and socializing at Patmore's, and fraternizing with the opposite sex.

Yet, although Shine and Fred are basically both black, the degrees of their colour ensures that socially they are unlikely to meet and in Shine's eyes Merrit and his like are as much the 'enemy' as is white America represented by Miss Cramp—the frail reminder of how America 'proper' perceives its black citizens.

Rudolph Fisher uses the biblical Jericho walls as a metaphor for racially divided America, both in a physical sense in terms of location, as well as in social interaction and spiritually. The 'walls of Jericho' are what separate the 'fays' (white people), 'dickties' (people of mixed-race heritage) and 'boogys' (ordinary black people)—'walls' erected to protect Americans from the 'pain and stress' of emotional contact.

The Walls of Jericho then, is not just a story about the Harlem of the twenties. Rudolph Fisher masterfully juxtaposes his characters and themes into a sparklingly witty tragi-comedy, which is as relevant in Britain now as it was in the Harlem Renaissance.

JUSTINA WOKOMA
author of *Acts of Inspiration*

INTRODUCTION

BELATEDLY, but with increasing and rewarding interest, America is beginning to acknowledge, identify, and re-evaluate its ample stock of cultural assets. Easily one of the most vital movements was the Harlem Renaissance, the period in the 1920s that witnessed explosive bursts of artistic creativity from black America. The genesis of the Renaissance has not yet been fully documented, but, among other things, the period echoed, with certain basic modifications, the frenzied pace of the Roaring Twenties. It attracted, from across the country and from many parts of the world, all kinds of curious and ambitious people, scholars and students, philanthropists and primitivists, but especially black artists—singers, dancers, sculptors, poets, writers—such as Paul Robeson, Bojangles Robinson, Bessie Smith, James Weldon Johnson, Langston Hughes and Alain Locke, the Harvard-trained Ph.D. and Rhodes scholar from Pennsylvania, who, in 1925, was the editor of the important anthology, *The New Negro*. Prominent white personalities included Salvador Dali, Somerset Maugham, Covarrubias, Clarence Darrow and Carl Van Vechten, whose articles in *Vanity Fair* and novel, *Nigger Heaven* (1926), stimulated even more white interest. Many of these artists congregated at fashionable Harlem nightclubs, wild 'rent parties', or in 'The Dark Tower' of Mrs A'Lelia Walker Robinson, Harlem heiress of the Madame Walker fortunes.

Aware all along that many whites were concerned only with sustaining black stereotypes, community leaders founded their own journals in which their writers would project other aspects of black America. Thus, W.E.B. Du Bois founded and edited *The Crisis*, the journal of the N.A.A.C.P., while A. Philip Randolph edited *The Messenger* for political radical action, and

Charles S. Johnson edited *Opportunity*, the organ of the Urban League. But although many were educated at Ivy League universities, the writers were different people, and they chose, to the despair or joy of various editors, different levels of black society. Some chose to present the 'respectable Negro', while others, like Rudolph Fisher, chose to depict the Harlem 'black folk' character.

Rudolph Fisher was one of those very creative people who live unfortunately brief, fast-paced lives. Born in 1897 in Washington, D.C., he was educated in the public schools of New York and Providence, Rhode Island, where his father was a minister. Fisher was a brilliant student at Brown University, where he switched from a major in English literature to biology, and earned keys to three national honour societies, Phi Beta Kappa, Sigma Xi, and Delta Sigma Rho, before he received his B.A. (1919) and M.A. (1920). While accompanying and arranging music for Paul Robeson on concert tours, Fisher took his M.D. from Howard University and in 1924 married Jane Ryder, a Washington school teacher. They moved to New York, where he studied at Columbia, practiced roentgenology, was superintendent of International Hospital, and at the same time, developed a deserved reputation as an outstanding short-story writer. While in pursuit of these several careers, Fisher became ill and was taken from his home in Jamaica, Long Island, to the Edgecombe Sanitorium, where he died in December 1934.

Fisher's literary output was considerable and widely published. Stories appeared in such publications as *The Crisis* ('High Yaller' in 1925), *The Atlantic Monthly* ('City of Refuge' and 'Ring Tail' in 1925, 'The Promised Land' and 'Blades of Steel' in 1927), *Opportunity* ('Guardian of the Law' in 1933) and *Story Magazine* ('Miss Cynthie' in 1933). There was a piece ('The Caucasian Storms Harlem' in 1927) in *American Mercury Magazine*, professional articles in *The Journal of Infectious Diseases*, and two novels, *The Walls of Jericho* (1928) and *The Conjure-Man Dies* (1932). The latter was produced as a folk play by the Federal Theatre Project's Negro Unit in 1936.

Always a realistic satirist, Fisher was very much aware of the pseudo-modishness, the cruel hypocrisy of much of the Harlem Renaissance—for instance, the average Harlem resident of the time was not allowed into the fashionable, white-owned and white-attended nightclubs in his own community. Fisher's fictional themes are varied, but he seems to be most concerned with the outcome of confrontations between big city corrosiveness and newly urbanized 'rural' black people. He may have indulged some romantic primitivism in *The Conjure-Man Dies*, but generally, as in 'The South Lingers On', a sensitive five-part sketch, he is sincere in reflecting the folk life around him.

While colour-consciousness destroys a romance in 'High Yaller', colour does not seem pivotally important in most of his other short stories. Written on a bet that no one short novel could blend the extremes of Harlem society into a single cohesive story successfully, *The Walls of Jericho* is an especially comprehensive display of the themes that are common in American black literature and Fisher's own brilliantly satirical treatment of such themes. Thus, colour (with the lawyer, Merrit), the well-intentioned but hopelessly uncomprehending white philanthropist (Miss Agatha Cramp), the antics of the conveniently paired stock 'folk' characters (Jinx and Bubber), the ultimate triumph of the put upon, honest and simple black guy (Shine), the pretensions of the educated avant garde (The Litter Rats) and other literary ploys are all presented here for inspection and enjoyment. Students of American black literature, and the Harlem Renaissance especially, will find the book important for even more reasons.

WILLIAM H. ROBINSON, Jr.
Professor of English
Howard University

For Glendora—

*May her laugh be silver,
like her hair*

CONTENTS

Joshua fit d' battle of Jericho
And d' walls come tumblin' down—

JERICHO

CHAPTER I

DESPITE the objections of the dickties, who prefer to ignore the existence of so-called rats, it is of interest to consider Henry Patmore's Pool Parlour on Fifth Avenue in New York.

The truth about Fifth Avenue has only half been told—that it harbours an aristocracy of residence already yielding to an aristocracy of commerce. Has any New Yorker confessed to the rest—that when aristocratic Fifth Avenue crosses One Hundred Tenth Street, leaving Central Park behind, it leaves its aristocracy behind as well? Here are bargain stores, babble, and kids, dinginess, odours, thick speech. Fallen from splendour and doubtless ashamed, the Avenue burrows into the ground and plunges beneath a park which hides it from One Hundred Sixteenth to One Hundred Twenty-fifth Street. Here it emerges moving uncertainly northward a few more blocks; and now— irony of ironies—finds itself in Negro Harlem.

You can see the Avenue change expression from blankness to horror then conviction. You can almost see it wag its head in self-commiseration. Not just because this is Harlem—there are proud streets in Harlem: Seventh Avenue of a Sunday afternoon, Strivers' Row, and The Hill. Fifth Avenue's shame lies in having missed these so-called dicky sections, in having poked its head out into the dark kingdom's backwoods. A city jungle this, if ever there was one, peopled largely by untamed creatures that live and die for the moment only. Accordingly, here strides melodrama, naked and unashamed.

Patmore's Pool Parlour occupied the remodelled ground floor of a once elegant apartment-house: two long low adjacent rooms, with a smaller one in the rear. You could enter either of the larger two from the street, and a doorway joined them within. There were no pretences about these two rooms: one was a pool room, its green-covered tables extending from front to back in a long squat row, the other was a saloon, with a mahogany bar counter, a great wall mirror, a shining foot rail and brass spittoons. In the saloon you could get any drink you had courage and cash enough to order, in the pool room you could play for any stake and use any language you had the ingenuity to devise. The third room was off the pool room and behind the saloon, this gave itself over to that triad of swift exchange, poker, blackjack, and dice.

Such was Pat's standing in the community that you might at any time find in this little rear room a policeman sitting in a card game, his coat on the back of his chair, his cap on the back of his head. For men, Pat's was supremely the neighbourhood's social centre, where you met real regular guys and rubbed elbows with authority. Henry Patmore was no piker, no sir, not by a damn sight.

In Patmore's the discussion concerned a possible riot in Harlem, a popular topic among these men who loved battle.

Jinx Jenkins and Bubber Brown led the argument on opposite sides, reinforced by continuous expressions of vague but hearty agreement from their partisans:

'Tell him 'bout it!'

'That's the time, papa!'

'There now, shake that one off yo' butt!'

Jinx and Bubber worked at the same job every day, moving furniture. At this they got along tolerably, but after hours they were chronic enemies and were absolutely unable to agree upon anything.

Jinx was thin and elongated, habitually stooped in bearing, lean and sinewy, with freckled skin of a slick deep yellow and a chronically querulous voice.

'Fays got better sense,' said he. 'Never will be no riot no mo' 'round hyeh.'

Bubber was as different from Jinx as any man could be, short, round and bulging, with a complexion bordering on the invisible.

'It isn't due to be 'round hyeh,' he corrected. 'It's way over Court Avenue way. Darkey's go'n' move in there tomorrow and fays jes' ain't gon' stand fo' it.' Bubber spoke with a loose-lipped lisp, perfected by the absence of upper incisors.

'Who he?' Jinx inquired.

'Some lawyer 'n other named Merrit.'

'The one got Pat in that mess with d' gover'ment?'

'Nobody else,' said Bubber.

'Well if he's a lawyer he sho' mus' know what he's doin'.'

'Don' matter what he is,' argued Bubber. 'If he move in that neighbourhood, fays'll start sump'm sho', and sho' as they start it, d' boogies'll finish it. Won't make no difference 'bout this Merrit man—he'll jes' be d' excuse— Man, you know that. Every sence d' war, d' boogys is had guns and ammunition they stole from d' army, and they jes' dyin' fo' a chance to try 'em out. I know where they's two machine guns myself, and they mus' be a hundred mo' in Harlem.'

'Yea,' said Jinx. 'I've heard 'bout that, too. But I don't think no shine's got no business busting into no fay neighbourhood.'

'He got business busting in any place he want to go. Only way for him to get anywhere is to bust in—ain't nobody go'n' *invite* him in.'

'Aw, man, what you talkin' 'bout? He's a dicky trying his damnedest to be like all the other dickties. When they get in hot water they all come cryin' to you and me fo' help.'

'And they get help, what I mean. Any time dickties start fightin', d' rest of us start fightin' too. Got to. Dickties can't fight.'

'Jus' 'cause they can't fight ain't no reason how come we got to fight for him.'

''Tain't nothin' else. Fays don't see no difference 'tween dickty shines and any other kind o' shines. One jig in danger is every jig in danger. They'd lick *them* and come on down on *us*. Then we'd have to fight anyhow. What's use o' waitin'?'

'Damned if you'd ever go out o' yo' way to fight for no dickties,' Jinx taunted.

'Don't know, I might,' Bubber said.

'Huh!' discredited Jinx. 'You wouldn't go out o' yo' way to fight for y' own damn self—and you're far from a dickty.'

'Right,' cheerfully agreed Bubber. 'I'm far from a dickty, no lie. But I ain't so far from a rat.' Jinx missed the meaning of this, so Bubber sidled up close to him and drove it home. 'Fact I'm right next to one.'

Encircling grins improved Jinx's understanding. 'Next to nuthin'!' he exploded, giving the other a rough push.

'Next to nuthin', then,' acquiesced Bubber, caroming off. 'You know what you is lots better'n I do.' Whereupon he did a triumphant little buck and wing step, which ended in a single loud, dust-raising stamp. Dry dust and drier laughter floated irritatingly into Jinx's face. Jinx was long and limber but his restraint was short and brittle. Derision snapped it in two.

'So's yo' whole damn family nuthin'!' he glowered, heedless of the disproportion between the trivial provocation and so violent a reaction. For it is the gravest of insults, this so-called 'slipping in the dozens'. To disparage a man himself is one thing, to disparage his family is another. 'Slipping' is a challenge holding all the potentialities of battle. The present example of it brought Bubber up short and promptly withdrew the bystanders' attention from their gin.

The bystanders began 'agitatin''—uttering comments deliberately intended to urge the two into action. The agitators concealed their grins far up their sleeves, presenting countenances grave with apprehension and speaking in tones resigned to the inevitability of battle.

'Uh-uh! Sho' mus' know each other well!'

'Where I come from, they fights fo' less than that.'

'If y' can't stand kiddin', don't kid, I say.'

'I don't believe he's going hit him, though.'

'I know what I'd do if anybody said that about my family.'

As a matter of fact, the habitual dissension between these two was the symptom of a deep affection which neither, on question, would have admitted. Neither Jinx and Bubber nor any of their associates had ever heard of Damon and Pythias, and frank regard between two men would have been considered questionable to say the least. Their fellows would neither have understood nor tolerated it; would have killed it by derisions, conjectures, suggestions, comments banishing the association to some realm beyond normal manhood. Accordingly their own expression of this affection had to take an ironic turn. They themselves must deride it first, must hide their mutual inclination in a garment of constant ridicule and contention, the irritation of which rose into their consciousness as hostility. Words and gestures which in a different order of life would have required no suppression became with them necessarily inverted, found issue only by assuming a precisely opposite aspect, concealed a profound attachment by exposing an extravagant enmity. And this was a distortion of behaviour so completely imposed upon them by their traditions and society that even they themselves did not know they were masquerading.

Bubber, his round face gone ominously blank, drew slowly closer to Jinx, who, face thrust forward a little and scowling, stood with his back to the bar counter, on which both elbows rested.

'Mean—*my* family?' inquired Bubber.

Jinx dared not recant. 'All the way back to the apes,' he assured him '—and that ain't so awful far back.'

'The apes in yo' family is still livin',' said Bubber, 'but there's go'n' be one dead in a minute.'

'Stay where you at, you little black balloon, or I'll stick a pin in you, you hear?'

By this time Bubber was almost within range and an initial blow was imminent. Absorbed in the impending clash, no one had noticed the arrival of a newcomer. But now this newcomer spoke and his words, soft and low though they were, commanded immediate attention.

'Winner belongs to me.'

Everybody looked—spectators holding their drinks, Bubber with his blank black face, Jinx with his murderous scowl. They saw a man at one end of the bar counter, one foot raised upon the brass rail, one elbow resting on the mahogany ledge, a young man so tall that, though he bent forward from the hips in a posture of easy nonchalance, he could still see over every intervening head between himself and the two opponents, and yet so broad that his height was not of itself noticeable; a supremely tranquil young Titan, with a face of bronze, hard, metallic, lustrous, profoundly serene. He repeated his remark in paraphrase:

'I am askin' fo' the winner. I am very humbly requestin' a share in his hind-parts.'

It was apparent that the bristling antagonists bristled no longer, had limply lost interest in their quarrel.

'Aw, man,' mumbled Jinx, 'what you talkin' 'bout?'

'You know what I'm talkin' 'bout you freckle-faced giraffe, and so does that baby hippopotamus in front of you. We got that Court Avenue job in the mornin', and if I've got to break in one rooky on it, I might as well break in two.' The voice, too, was like bronze, heavy, rich in tone, uncompromisingly solid, with a surface shadowy and smooth as velvet save for an occasional ironic glint.

'This boogy,' explained Bubber, 'thinks he's bad. Come slippin' me 'bout my family. He knows I don't play nuthin' like that.'

'Needn't get uppity 'bout it,' mumbled Jinx sullenly.

'Ain't gettin' uppity. Jus' naturally don't like it, that's all. Keep yo' thick lips off my family if y' know what's good fo' you.'

He who had interrupted queried blandly, 'Ain't there go'n' be no fight?'

Jinx said to Bubber, 'Aw go ahead, drabble-tail. Ain't nobody studyin' yo' family.'

And this questionable apology Bubber chose to accept. 'Oh,' said he. 'Oh—aw right, then. That's different.'

The atmosphere cleared, attention returned to gin and jest, and Bubber approached the giant, who now was grinning.

'Certainly am sorry there ain't go'n' be no hostilities,' sighed the latter. 'Been wantin' to spank yo' little black bottom ever since you broke that rope this mornin'.'

'Aw go ahead, Shine. That boogy's shoutin' because you was here to protect him. I'm go'n' to catch him one these days when you ain't 'round, and I'm go'n' turn him every way but loose.'

'Don't let him surprise you. He can wrestle the hell out of a piano.'

'Piano don't fight back.'

'Don't it? Well—neither will you if he gets the same hold on you.'

'Humph. Who the hell's scared o' that freckle-faced giraffe?'

CHAPTER II

PATMORE, the proprietor, appeared. A large, powerful man with a broad, hard face, a bright display of gold teeth, and the complexion of a guinea hen's egg. He wore a loose brown suit, of which the coat was large and boxy and the ample trousers sharply creased but so long that they broke about his ankles in cubistic planes and angles. Smoke and the caustic vapours of rum had rendered his voice rough and husky, and when he spoke you had an irresistible impulse to clear your throat.

Pat addressed Bubber. 'You and Long-Boy still at it, huh?'

'Aw, that string-bean's crazy. I'm go'n' snap him in two and string him one these times.'

'Know what I'm go'n' do with you two?'

'What?'

'See that door over there?'

'Yea.'

'That's the cellar door, see? Next time y' all start anything in here, I'm going to send the two of you down there and let you settle it once and for. all. Best man come out—other one drug out. See?'

'Any rats down there?'

'Yea, and y'all 'll make two more.'

'Well,' grinned Bubber, 'when I walk out, them rats'll have some bones to gnaw on anyhow,' and he moved off toward the pool room.

Ignoring Pat's attempt to play the genial host. Shine had already returned to his drink with an indifference hardly short of insult. He now replenished his glass from a pint bottle in his hand, and slipped the bottle into his own hip pocket.

Pat's green eyes narrowed. 'That'll be only three bucks to you, Shine.'

Shine looked up. 'What?'

'Anybody else—four.'

'This,' said Shine, 'is *good* liquor.'

"Course 'tis. All my liquor is good.'

'This ain't never been yourn 'scription liquor.' Shine sampled his glass with an odd mingling of relish and unconcern, the one unmistakably for his drink, the other for his company.

Pat feigned incredulity. 'Mean that's *your* liquor?'

"Tain't my brother's.'

'Mean—' Pat's unbelief mounted '—mean you buy liquor somewhere else and bring it in my place to drink?'

Shine tossed off the rest of the glass, set it down on the bar counter, and looked upon Pat, who was almost as tall as himself, with a wearily tolerant smile.

'Sho' takes you a long time to see a thing,' he remarked. 'You hear me say it's 'scription. You ain't runnin' no drugstore, are y'? You see me drink it. You ain't blind, are y'? Yea, I bought it. Yea, I brought it here. Yea, I'm drinking it. Now what the hell 'bout it?'

A smaller man equally 'bad', equally convinced of the necessity of being hard, but aware of physical odds against him, would have said this with sneers and sarcasm, thus bolstering his courage against his handicap. Shine however had never found it necessary to be nasty as well as bad. He had spoken with an air of amusement, and there was but a touch of challenge in his terminal remark.

Pat stood silent a moment. Eventually he said: 'Nothin' 'bout it, big boy. Nothin'. Jes' askin' fo' information, that's all.' And rather too abruptly he walked away.

Shine stared long into his third glass of 'scription liquor before he lifted it to his lips. Good whiskey is not like gin. Gin makes you forget, good whiskey makes you remember. Perhaps it was at the memories in this, his third glass of good whiskey, that Shine now stared . . .

A boy, overgrown, bigger by far than his fellow orphan asylu-mites, so much bigger that they never challenged him to do battle as they frequently challenged the others. As big, almost, as the superintendent, about whom the smallest thing was his pebble of a heart. They were all at work in the truck garden, Shrimpie, Frankfurter, Jellybean and the others, as well as this overgrown one whose name was then Joshua Jones. They were picking tomatoes, mostly green ones, to be taken to the kitchen and made into 'pickalilly'. They were seeing who could pick most in the hour allotted to them for the work.

And Shrimpie, unaware that they were being watched from the window of the nearest cottage, suddenly stopped, staring in surprise and delight at a big, red, prematurely ripe tomato in his hand.

'Y'all can work as fast as you please,' Shrimpie declared. 'I'm go'n' stop and eat this here one.'

Three bites out of the luscious thing—and the superinten-dent's hand was on Shrimpie's shoulder. Three cruelly vehement shakes of Shrimpie's little body—and a hard green tomato sped through space and broke on the super's cheek.

The red face became redder, the super dropped Shrimpie and turned toward the big boy, enraged. Made for him—dodged another tomato—came on. Grappled, scuffled, slipped, fell, and found the boy astride him. Pounding on his head—pounding—gone quite crazy, pounding. The super was stunned less by the pounding than by the fact that the boy kept doing it. Even after he was shaken off, the boy kept fighting aggressively. Without a rod it wasn't so easy to tame an overgrown sixteen-year-old devil. When they both let up, it was at least spiritually Joshua Jones's round.

A bigger boy now, almost a man; well over six feet tall, but still ribby and hungry-looking. Eighteen now. Shining shoes in front of a Lenox Avenue barber-shop. Making nine, ten, sometimes twelve dollars a week.

The head barber liked to stand in the doorway and kid the boy about being so big.

'Great big husky—' he would draw out the 'great' till it was as long as Joshua himself—'great big husky like you—it's a shame. You oughter be movin' pianos 'stead o' whippin' shoe-leather. Benny, come here. Look at dis boy. When he stoop over, his heels is higher 'n his head.'

Joshua Jones took it good naturedly, grinned occasionally, said little. 'Shine?' was the most he ever uttered, and from this the men dubbed him Shine.

Nobody called him Shine, however, but Negroes. A fay patron, with no other intent than to be genial, once repeated the name Shine after hearing the head barber use it. 'How do you get to the subway from here, Shine, my boy?' he asked, paying his bill.

Shine looked him up and down, and after a moment inquired, 'How 'd you know my name was Shine?'

'Guessed it,' smiled the patron.

'Guess how to get to the subway, then.'

The patron stared, gaped and departed mystified at so sudden hostility.

But the head barber, looking on, grinned and approved. 'Tight kid,' he commented. 'What I mean, *tight.*'

A tight kid makes a hard man—two hundred and twenty pounds of hardness in this case, wrestling daily with pianos, pianos equally hard and four times as heavy; two hundred and twenty pounds of strength, not the mere strength of stevedores hooking cotton bales on a wharf; you can't hurt a bale of cotton—it can't hurt you; tumble it, hook it, kick it—what the hell? But pianos— even swaddled in quilting—pianos must be handled like glass. Not mere strength do they require, but delicacy and strength, not muscles driving out or yanking in with abandoned force, but muscles held taut, precisely controlled under however great tension, released or restrained at will. You are protecting not only the instrument but yourself and your partner at the other end. The soft edge of a cotton-bale won't hurt a fellow's foot—the hard one of a piano will break it.

A piano is a malicious thing, it loves to slip out of your grip and snap at your toes, with an evil chuckle inside. Push up its lip and see it sneer; touch it and hear it rumble or whine. Ponderous, spiteful, treacherous live thing—a single spirit in a thousand bodies, one of which will crush you soon or late.

A malicious thing. Only today they were putting a piano into a third-storey window of a house on a busy street. They had used hooks over the cornice, and the cheap rotten cement crumbled. Cornices aren't supposed to bear weight—an inferior mixture will do. One hook came through just as Shine was reaching out of the window to catch hold of the suspended instrument and guide it through the frame. He heard the crackle of broken cement above, saw the instrument sag a little while over it showered crumbs of broken cornice. With the hand already extended he grabbed the nearest leg of the upright and pulled it part way through the window just before the other hook lost its hold above. The greater part of the piano however was still unsupported outside the window—the longer arm of a lever that all but broke even Shine's tremendous strength. Straining back with all the power of his back and arms, his knees braced against the lower edge of the window-frame, he held the instrument there slipping on the sill till Jinx and Bubber reached him. Someone must have been hurt in the crash that would surely have come otherwise.

'Thing nearly pulled me out the window,' he remarked when the piano was again under control.

'Why the hell didn't y' let it go, then?'

Shine looked rather blank. 'Damn' if I thought of it,' he said and grinned at his own stupidity.

CHAPTER III

JOSHUA JONES, whom his fellows called Shine, came out of his reverie to observe the return of Jinx and Bubber, arm in arm and quite happily drunk.

'This yeh freckle-faced giraffe, he's a good boogy,' Bubber declared. 'Good boogy, yessir. He's my boy. Ain't you my boy, biggy?'

'No lie,' Jinx agreed. 'Tell 'im 'bout that liquor we ruined.'

'Try some good liquor,' Shine invited, turning the rest of his pint over to them. 'Go 'head—I got enough.'

'Jes' had some good liquor, I tell y'—Pat saw us go—'

'Y'all drink,' Shine ordered, 'and let me do the talkin'.'

'Talk, then—talk. Don' nobody have to listen jes' 'cause you talk. Talk.'

'I told y'all 'bout that Court Avenue job in the mornin'.'

'What d' hell you so worried 'bout that job for?'

'Might have to get me some extra hands. Boss told me find somebody.'

There was quick and sober resentment on the part of Jinx and Bubber. 'Extra hands—fo' what? Ain't no job too big fo' us three.'

'Trouble, maybe,' Shine explained. 'You know what's happened already. Guy tried to move in on One Hundred Forty-ninth Street this winter and they dared 'em to take the stuff out of the van. Jes' last month, four blocks from where we go tomorrow, somebody put dynamite under a shine that moved in on his hardness. Well, boss is making this dickty pay for risk this time, and we get a bonus, see? But we got to get the stuff in safe, else—no bonus. And we got to keep our eyes open, or we may leave some of our hips right up there on that Court Avenue asphalt.'

'Won't leave none o' Jinx's,' Bubber prophesied.

'How come?' challenged Jinx.

'Because you ain't got none to leave, you doggone eel.'

'So be ready for anything,' Shine said. 'Five bucks extra apiece if the junk gets in o.k.'

'Well—' Bubber was uncertain, '—five bucks is five bucks, but they's a lot mo' five buckses loose in the world 'n there is hips. Look yeh.' He exhibited his own hips by drawing his coat in tight around the waist. 'See them? It's took me twenty-five years to get them. And you talking 'bout lettin' somebody throw dynamite at 'em fo' five bucks. Huh. Man down at Coney Island once offered me *ten* bucks a day jes' to let 'em throw baseballs at my head—and baseballs don't explode.'

'Furthermo',' Jinx added, 'you could spare that head. 'Twouldn't be no loss whatsoever.'

'Point is,' said Shine, 'five bucks or nothin', I'm jes' tellin' y' to be ready, see? If anybody bother us jes' up and knock hell out 'n 'em, that's all.'

'You a pretty hard boogy, Mr Shine,' Bubber observed, 'but I ain't never see you knock the hell out 'n no dynamite.'

'Far as I'm concerned,' contributed Jinx, 'I'm ready now—to run. I been haulin' furniture, and I been haulin' pianos; but when they starts plantin' dynamite, this baby's go'n' start haulin' hind-parts!'

'Be the first honest haulin' you ever done, too,' commented Bubber.

To Shine this banter was merely a pledge of allegiance in case of crisis, assurance that the hiring of extra hands would in no event be necessary. Beneath the jests, the avowed fear, the merriment, was a characteristic irony, a typical disavowal of fact and repudiation of reality, a markedly racial tendency to make light of what actually was grave—a tendency stressed in Jinx and Bubber by the habitual perversion of their own conduct toward each other. Members of another race might have said simply:

'What the hell do you think we are—quitters?'

So between them they killed the rest of the pint and mourned its death with laughter.

Patmore returned, grinning.

'You two,' he directed Bubber and Jinx, 'catch air. I got a bug to put in the big boy's ear.' And when they had eventually obeyed, he went on to Shine: 'Jes' to show y' there's no hard feelin's, I got a scheme that means bucks, and if you got two good eyes, you can see how to make some of 'em.'

'There's mo' guys in jail for schemin' than there is for bein' blind.'

'Listen. You don't specially like no dickties, do y'?'

'I ain't none too fond o' rats.'

'But dickties give you a very special pain, don't they?'

'Lots o' places. No lie.'

'Me too. Now that's where you and I are alike, see?'

Shine's silence admitted nothing; but Pat went on:

'Heard you say sump'm 'bout movin' this dickty Merrit.'

'Did?'

'Yea. Now there's a guy I can't see with field glasses.'

'No?'

'No. Tell you sump'm.' Pat looked about to be sure of privacy, leaned closer to the bar counter. 'If Merrit died tomorrer—I wouldn't send 'im no flowers.'

'What you got 'gainst 'im?'

'Plenty.' There came a characteristic confidential twist to one side of Pat's mouth. 'He put me in some time back, see? Damage suit—ten thousand berries. Hit a guy crossin' the speedway—knocked him for a gool, the dumbbell. Well—it was pay off or see jail, and naturally I wasn't go'n' see jail. Coulda' got out cheaper maybe, only this bird Merrit wouldn't listen to reason. Claim' he was go'n' bring in my occupation and lots o' other stuff if I didn't come clean—forcin' my hand, see? Knew I had cash and knew he could make me pay off by threatenin' to squeal. I ought to 'a' crowned 'im then, but he was too wise, knew where to meet me and when. So all I could do was pay off. Ten thousand bucks to stay out o' jail.'

'Ten thousand bucks wasted,' Shine said.

Pat misunderstood. 'Yea,' he agreed. 'Nothin' to show for it. Know what I could 'a' done with that much at that time?'

'What?'

'I could 'a' bought in a fay neighbourhood and held on for a price. I could 'a' made fifteen thousand on that ten. Same as he's doin' now.'

'So now you figure on a come-back?'

Pat was almost reproachful. ''Course not—that ain't the kind o' bird I am. Hell, I ain't evil, Shine. Anyway there ain't nothin' I can do about it now anyhow, is there?'

'How'n the hell do I know?'

'All I want is his trade, man. Bygones can be bygones, far as I give a damn. Gettin' even is woman's stuff—man don't hold no grudges. But if I can sell him and his friends liquor regular, it'll mean a lot to me, see?'

'Unscheme yo' scheme, boogy.'

'Listen. I'm handlin' a Canadian Club that'll sell itself, no stuff. If I can get him to sample it, he'll take it—order it for himself and recommend it to his friends. It's bound to go big, see? But here's the thing: if he knows I sent it he'll figure I'm tryin' to poison him and be scared to touch it, see? Now I got half a case on hand he can have and I got ten bucks you can have if you deliver it along with his things in the mornin'.'

Shine's brows lifted. 'Yea?'

'Yea. You're my agent, see? Only don't tell him—let him think you're handlin' it yourself. There'll be more later—not only to him but his friends, and you can collect every time. How 'bout it?'

Shine's answer did not come promptly.

'Fact,' Pat pursued, 'with yo' job, you could work up a

wonderful delivery service for me—no suspicion attached to it, see? Here's yo' chance, man—start out as my agent.'

'Agent yo' hiney,' said Shine. 'Listen. Ain't you heard 'bout me?'

''Bout you?'

'Sho', man. I done started already.'

'Bootleggin'?'

'No lie. I got a regular business. Ain't but two people in it, though, the bootlegger and the customer. I'm both of 'em.'

Once again Pat eyed Shine in silent frustration and, after an angry moment, turned away wordless.

Watching him go, Shine grinned, then frowned and muttered to himself:

'Wise guy. Aimin' to choke Merrit and throw the blame on me. Jes' 'cause I bring my own liquor in and pass up his kerosene. Can y' beat it? Wonder how many kinds of a jackass that bozo thinks I am?'

CHAPTER IV

By way of contrast, it is of further interest to drop in on a little group of dickties, superiorly self-named the Litter Rats, who were assembled informally this evening in the dwelling of one J. Pennington Potter, their current president.

This particular meeting of the Litter Rats' Club had been set apart for the discussion of The Negro's Contribution to Art and The Lost Sciences of Ethiopia. But when Fred Merrit announced that he had bought a house on Court Avenue, most exclusive of the residential streets adjacent to Negro Harlem, scheduled discussions were for the moment forgotten; and when he added that he intended to live in the house, and to do so whether a riot resulted or not, the dozen men about the room came promptly to the edges of their chairs.

'Preposterous!' said J. Pennington Potter, a plump little sausage of a man, whose skin seemed stuffed to the limit with the importance of what it contained.

'Why so?' inquired Merrit.

'This colony,' Potter pronounced, 'should extend itself naturally and gradually—not by violence and bloodshed.'

'The extension of territory by violence and bloodshed strikes me as natural enough,' Merrit grinned. 'I haven't much of a memory, but I seem to recall one or two instances—'

'Progress is by evolution, not revolution,' expostulated J. Pennington Potter. 'And you may be sure that race progress is no exception.'

'Who the deuce said anything about race progress or about extending the colony?' asked Tod Bruce, the young and far from fundamentalist rector of St Augustine's. 'Why is it that a shine can never do anything except as a shine?'

'Well,' commented Langdon, an innocent looking youngster

who was at heart a prime rascal and who compensated by writing poetry, 'if Fred will just keep his hat on, none of his neighbours will know he's a shine.'

'Or he could try Stay-Straight for those kinks—' someone suggested.

'My point,' said Bruce, 'is that Fred probably isn't concerned primarily with the racial aspect of the thing—'

'He ought to be!' exploded Potter.

'I am,' said Merrit coolly. 'All of you know where I stand on things racial—I'm downright rabid. And even though, as Tod suggests, I'd enjoy this house, if they let me alone, purely as an individual, just the same I'm entering it as a Negro. I hate fays. Always have. Always will. Chief joy in life is making them uncomfortable. And if this doesn't do it—I'll quit the bar.'

'Well, Fred,' said Langdon, 'don't forget the revenue. They'll pay you double the value of the place just to get you out, you know.'

'I had that in mind, but hell—what's money? They won't pay me what I'll ask anyhow, and I won't sell for less.'

There was a certain grimness about Merrit, for all his rosy cheeks and cherubic grin. He was anomalous in certain important particulars. Fair as the northernmost Nordic, his sandy hair was yet as kinky as that of any pure blooded African; and not the blackest of Negroes could have hated the dominant race more thoroughly.

'You know,' he said, 'I especially wanted my mother to live there. How she would have queened it—it would have been part compensation—'

It was another of Merrit's anomalies that, though he hated his lineage in general, he had been especially devoted to his mother. She had always seemed to him a symbol of sexual martyrdom, a bearer of the cross, as he put it, which fair manhood universally placed on dark womanhood's shoulders. Of all those whom he blamed and cursed for his own mongrel heritage, she was the one exception. For her, the only one he had actually known, he had only racial pity and filial devotion. She had recently died, late enough in her own life, but too early in his, to enjoy the luxuries he had just become able to give her. And so in addition to what she already represented, she had now become a symbol of motherhood unrewarded, idealized in memory far beyond what had been true in life.

'I think,' he added, 'my housekeeper will give the neighbours enough of a shock, though. She's as coloured as they come.'

'There'll be a riot!' exclaimed J. Pennington Potter.

'Good!' grinned the cherubic Fred.

'They'll set fire to the place, they'll blow it up—the way they did Morris and Peters.'

'Insurance is a marvellous invention, isn't it?'

'Uncalled for distress. I thoroughly disapprove of deliberate, intentional havoc. It's just what we're trying to prevent.' This was to be expected of the extremely proper Pennington Potter, a 'social worker' with a windy, pompous voice and a deep devotion to convention.

'Well,' moderated Bruce, 'Harlem began its growth by riots. I remember when I was a youngster, I used to be scared to stay out after dark. It was pretty bad then—either a crowd of fay boys would catch a jig and beat him up or else a crowd of jigs would get a fay boy and teach him the fear of the Lord. In either case the thing would be the first skirmish of a pitched battle somewhere on the frontier. The shines tricked a half dozen Irish lads into One Hundred Thirty-fourth Street one night, I remember, and two of them never came out. Cops—there weren't any black cops then—always went in threes at least. And I recall one day when twelve mounted policemen came galloping up One Hundred Thirty-fourth Street after one little West Indian ice-man—and galloped back without him. It was really comical.'

The others gave Bruce attention, watching him as he spoke. He too was fair, but less so than Merrit, and his skin was uniformly pallid. His face was lean, his features prominent and severe to the point of austerity, the nose large and narrow, the chin advancing, the mouth wide, straight and thin lipped. As if to offset the ascetic in this countenance, his eyes were deep-set and black, and in them some curious passion gleamed constantly like a flame. As he spoke these eyes engaged everything that might hold a drop of interest, comprehended it, drained it, left it; swiftly flashed from this to that, paused, penetrated, abandoned; sought further, halted, penetrated again, departed—a pair of black wasps.

'Those were the happy days,' he went on. 'People kept kettles of hot lye on the stoves and carried them to their doors whenever the bell rang. And you could go upon the roof of your house and not see a chimney within four blocks: they'd all been knocked down and the bricks stacked at front room windows for ammunition. And say one night a bunch of bad jigs—like those over on Fifth Avenue now—mistook me for a fay, and I had a devil of a time proving I was a Negro, too!'

'I had the same experience,' said Merrit. 'You should have seen me exhibiting my kinky head.'

'It was probably straight for a while,' grinned Langdon.

'It's the old, old story,' said Bruce. 'War—conquest of territory. But our side of the thing isn't all there is to it. The fays have a side too, you know.'

'I know,' Merrit protested, like the lawyer he was, 'but we aren't supposed to see that.'

'Well, I don't know. It's easy to laugh now. But the fact is, it was tragedy. Black triumph is always white tragedy. We won— we won territory. All the fays had to get out, make way, make room for us. What did they do? Resist, of course—why the devil shouldn't they? Clung to their district, tried to recover. And we broke their heads with chimney bricks and bathed their bodies in hot lye. How do you suppose they felt about it?'

'Best thing that ever happened to 'em,' grinned Fred.

'But tough on *them*, you'll admit.'

'What of it?'

'Only this—that when you move up there on Court Avenue, you're opening up all those old scars. Just as Pott says, they'll resist. They'll warn you with threatening notes. They'll try to buy you out. If these don't work, they will probably dynamite you.'

'I've received one warning already.'

'You have?'

'You heard about Gamby, last month,' said someone. 'They had a gang of toughs on hand and they wouldn't even let the movers land his stuff on the sidewalk. Had to get the police.'

'Glad you mentioned that,' said Merrit. 'I'll send my worst stuff first, and I'll get the toughest furniture-movers in Harlem.'

'Nowadays,' Bruce observed, 'we grow by, well, a sort of passive conquest. The fays move out, and the jigs are so close that no more fays will move in. So the landlord has to rent to jigs and the colony keeps extending. But if Fred wants to return to the older method, I don't think it will do any great harm to the rest of us. He's taking all the risk. And even though he claims a racial interest, he has admitted that the chief motive is personal after all. It's his business.'

'There is absolutely no excuse for it,' was J. Pennington Potter's final dictum.

'Who the hell asked for an excuse, Pott?' was all that Merrit answered.

CHAPTER V

COURT AVENUE is a straight, thin spinster of a street which even in July is cold. There is about it an air of arched eyebrows, of skirts drawn aside and comments made with a sniff. It is adorned in sparse, lean, scrawny maples, all suffering from malnutrition, and these tend to stress rather than relieve the hardness of dry, level pavements.

The dwellings are all the same pale grey and are all essentially alike, four storeys tall, thin to gauntness, droop-eyed with drawn shapes, standing shoulder to shoulder in long, inhospitable rows. Stone stoops, well withdrawn from the sidewalk, lend an air of inaccessibility, and the tiny front yards that might dispel this illusion by only a bit of grass or a flower are instead uniformly laid away beneath slabs of expressionless concrete.

Twice a day, when sunlight touches the windows of this side in the morning and again of that side at night, Court Avenue smiles a chilly, crystalline smile. It is the sort of smile that goes with the words, 'My dear! Can you imagine such a thing!' and you might suppose that the street was returning even the sun's genial greeting and warm farewell with a disapproving sneer.

In short, Court Avenue is a snob of a street. Yet it is somewhat to be pitied in its pretence at ignoring the punishment that is at hand: the terribly sure approach of the swiftly spreading Negro colony.

Isaacs' Transportation Company, which is to say old man Isadore Isaacs, would have trusted Joshua Jones with any moving job whatsoever. It was work that Shine loved because of the challenge it presented to his personal strength and skill. He took charge, accepted responsibility, helped execute the orders he gave. Whenever a staircase or hallway presented a difficult turn or an insufficient dimension, he was at hand to decide just how the problem should be solved. Whenever a valuable piece of ungainly size had to be dismembered, and afterwards reconstructed, his knowledge of the mysterious anatomy of furniture was wholly adequate. Whenever a piano was to be hoisted, he saw to each important item: himself selected and anchored the tackle and guided the instrument through the window that was chosen to admit it.

Pianos indeed, were his particular prey, his almost living archenemies. He personified them, and out of controlling them, handling them, directing them helpless through mid-air, he derived a satisfaction comparable to that of a tamer of beasts. There was a superstition that a piano would 'get' a man one time or another. Jinx and Bubber had both suffered injuries from instruments that slipped from their grips. But Shine laughed at this superstition, not because it was a superstition, but because he knew that he simply couldn't be 'had'.

Even the four-ton van was to Shine a beloved companion. He called her Bess, and Bess was the only thing on earth that he coveted. She was padded within and especially designed for the moving of things fine and fragile, her engine was responsive and smooth, her treads pneumatic, single in front, double in the rear. She rode like a private ambulance and she could make forty on a level. It was Shine's ambition one day to win her away from old man Isaacs.

The crew was usually made up only of Shine, Jinx and Bubber, and these three in two years of cooperation had come to work together in a fashion beyond fault-finding, carefully, quickly, punctually, untrailed by patrons complaints.

This early summer morning Shine swung Bess, loaded with Merrit's possessions, into the chilly Court Avenue atmosphere, and, with deliberate malice, sped up to a roar, then coasted, shifting his spark to make the motor spit.

'That'll wake up somebody,' he grinned as Bess bang-banged

like an automatic. 'Come on you bomb-throwers, do your stuff—
let's go!'

'Boy, lemme out this cab,' said Bubber. 'This darkey done
gone crazy.'

'Shuh!' complained Jinx. 'Ain't go'n' be no rough stuff in this
neighbourhood. Deader than Strivers' Row.'

They drew up and backed against the kerb before number
three-thirteen. The door opened and Merrit himself came out
to meet them. He wore his usual air of nonchalance and his
usual cherubic grin.

'Hello, fellows,' he greeted. 'Get it all on one load? That's
clever.'

All three stared. Such cordiality in a dickty was nothing short
of astonishing, and it put the suspicious workers immediately
on guard.

While Jinx and Bubber unfastened van-doors, Merrit went
up to Shine and leaned carelessly against a tree. 'What do you
think of this?' he said, producing a letter.

Shine accepted the proffered note without enthusiasm. It
was without heading or salutation, typewritten, and lacking a
signature:

You are not wanted in this neighbourhood.
If you move in, we'll move you out.

'Where'd you get it?' Shine asked Merrit.

'Found it in the vestibule when I came up to look around
yesterday.'

'Humph,' said Shine. 'Jes' let 'em start sump'm while we're
here, that's all.' And because he disliked dickties and wanted
no talk with any one of them, he changed the subject rudely.
'Where you want us to put this stuff?'

'Anywhere. Spread it all over the first floor. My housekeeper
will come in from the country-place and have it arranged later.'

'Hear that?' Jinx said to Bubber, out of sight at the rear of the van. 'That's what I say 'bout a spade. Spade can't get a little sump'm without stretchin' it. His housekeeper. His country-place. Humph—what's a use lyin' like that?'

'He ain't lyin', fool. That jasper's got more bucks than you got freckles. Got a swell place on the upstate Pike, not far out o' town. Throws big parties and raises hell jes' like the fays. Folks up there didn't know he was a jig till he had a party—and they offered him a million dollars fo' the place jes' to get him out. He wouldn't leave, though.'

'Million dollars?'

'Uh-huh.'

'And he wouldn't leave?'

'Uh-huh.'

'Huh! You lie wuss'n he do.'

Merrit's words came to them repeating, 'Mrs Fuller will take care of everything later.'

'There now,' commented Jinx, 'y'see?'

'See what?'

'Soon as a old crow gets up in the world, he got to grab hisself some other guy's wife.'

Bubber regarded him with pity. 'How you figure that out?'

'*His* name ain't Fuller, is it?'

'No. And yo' name ain't Sherlock. Don't you know what a housekeeper is? And ain't you never heard of such a thing as a widow?'

'Aw man, what you talkin' 'bout?'

'You ought to be a policeman, brother.'

'How come?'

''Cause you very suspicious and very, very dumb.'

These two had been unwrapping carefully covered hindmost pieces of furniture. Shine came around to lend a hand, and Merrit moved along the kerb to a position such that he could observe them. Now he indulged in another astonishing speech.

'Don't be too damn careful about these things. Flat didn't

have anything but junk in it, anyway. Good stuff is in the country—won't move it in till fall. Just chuck this stuff in and let it lay.'

What manner of dickty was this? He greeted you like an equal, casually shared his troubles with you, and did not seem to care in the least what the devil you did with his furniture.

Jinx said sullenly to Bubber, 'All he wants is for us to scratch up something, so he can call the five bucks off.'

Bubber said to Jinx, 'That ain't it. He's jes' makin' sure o' friends in case the fays start sump'm.'

Shine said to himself, 'If this bird wasn't a dickty he'd be o.k. But there never was a dickty worth a damn.'

The job was finished and they were throwing by-products into the emptied van—burlap and canvas wrappers, quilting, hemp rope, leather straps. Merritt had just turned the key in his door and was facing about for departure, while Shine was on the point of climbing into the cab. At this juncture, simultaneously, everybody made an observation. It was the only observation that they all would have been likely to make at one time, and it held Merritt at attention on the stoop, rendered Shine motionless with one foot upon the step of his cab, and halted Bubber in the act of throwing a gunnysack over Jinx's head. Along the hitherto empty street a girl was briskly approaching.

You could see that she knew they were staring, so completely did she ignore them. And the ease with which she did so, the queenly unconcern with which she passed, indicated that she was accustomed to being stared at and did not mind it at all.

There was quite obviously no reason why she should have minded it. Certainly her attire invited no criticism—a brief frock of cool black satin, sheer gun-metal hose, and trim patent-leather pumps. Nor did she herself. She was tall and her face was pretty, and her body slenderly invited, though

her legs perversely eluded the persistent caress of the sedu-
lous soft black satin.

Even if this had been all—a pretty girl on that gaunt empty
street at this solitary hour, the staring would have been pardon-
able. But there was in addition an especially extenuating
circumstance: the girl was not white.

Before she quite passed beyond earshot Jinx and Bubber
were indulging in low enthusiasms:

'Boy, do you see what I see?'

'Law-aw-aw-dy!'

'Mus' be havin' a recess in heaven!'

'No lie. Umh-umh-umh—' Grunts to signify admiration far
beyond words.

'Lady, you can have all my week's pay—ev'ry bit of it.' Bubber
dived elaborately into his empty pockets, while Jinx vowed:

'I'm going get religion and die so I can go to heaven and
meet that angel—yessir!'

Suddenly comment ceased. Only two doors beyond Merrit's
house the girl turned in, traversed the short cement walk,
mounted the stoop, unlocked and entered the front door.

Merrit raised his brows in a characteristic little expression
of surprise. Shine saw him do so and had a swift interpretation
for that expression:

'Figurin' on a jive already—the doggone dickty hound. Why
the hell dickties can't stick to their own women without messin'
around honest workin' girls—'

Bubber was rapturizing without restraint, 'Man—oh—man!
A honey with high yellow legs! And did you see that walk? That
gal walks on ball-bearin's, she do—everythin' moves at once.'
He illustrated his idea with head-wobblings, shoulder-rollings,
and loose backward protrusions and retractions of buttocks. 'See
what I mean? Tail-conscious, man, tail-conscious—'

You jes' a damn liar,' came unexpectedly from Shine. 'She
walks like what she is, a lady—and you talk like what you is, a
rat. Come on, it's getting' late—let's go from here.'

Whereupon Jinx looked at Bubber and Bubber looked at Jinx. Here was indeed something new, Shine championing a woman.

'Well, kiss my assorted peanuts!' ejaculated Bubber.

'Guess that's the dynamite,' was Jinx's dyspeptic surmise.

UPLIFT

CHAPTER VI

Miss Agatha Cramp had, among other things, a sufficiently large store of wealth and a sufficiently small store of imagination to want to devote her entire life to Service; in fact, to Social Service on a large scale. And because Miss Cramp took a very personal interest in her successive servants, it came about that this Social Service was directed towards definite racial groups. When her maid had been French, Miss Cramp had organized a club to assist rebuilding demolished French villages; when her maid had been Polish, she had taken up with the Society for the Aid of Starving Poland; and shortly after hiring a Russian girl, she became a member of the Russian Relief Committee.

Thus Miss Cramp had devoted the more recent years of her life to Service, and now, with a coloured maid on hand, she had no outlet for her urge. For two weeks she had been idle, and idleness drove her to distraction. She felt worse and worse day by day, until at last her doctor said what she paid him to say: that she was on the verge of a nervous breakdown and would simply have to go to bed and rest.

She rested three days; whereupon an ironic Court Avenue sun revealed to her something of which she had hitherto been unaware: her coloured maid, bringing in her breakfast, looked somehow amazingly pretty. And although Miss Cramp had no generous eye for beauty, she was so struck by the discovery of what hitherto had mysteriously escaped her that she was moved to exclaim:

'Why, Linda, what've you done to yourself? You look so nice this morning.'

Linda stood stiff in astonishment, eventually managing what might have been construed as a reply:

'You—feeling better, Miss Cramp?' The twinkle in the maid's eye escaped her mistress.

'I believe I am, Linda. I really believe I am.' Miss Cramp stared at the girl a while, then turned her attention to the tray just placed on her lap; inspected it, looked through it absently.

'Something else, Miss Cramp?' asked Linda.

'No. This is very nice, Linda. Very nice. But don't go. I want to talk to you. Something has just occurred to me.'

It had indeed. For fifteen years Miss Cramp had been devoting her life to the service of mankind. Not until now had the startling possibility occurred to her that Negroes might be mankind, too.

The bare statement is extravagant; the fact is not. The only Negroes Miss Cramp had ever spoken to were porters, waiters and house servants of acquaintances. These were the only ones of whose existence she had been even remotely aware. Negroes to her had been rather ugly but serviceable fixtures, devices that happened to be alive, dull instruments of drudgery, so observed, so accepted, so used, and so forgotten. Had all the dark-skinned folk in the country been blotted out by some specific selective destruction, Miss Cramp would not have missed them in the least, would not have been glad nor sorry, would have gone serenely on unaware, tchk-tchk-ing perhaps over the newspaper account, but remaining wholly untouched in her sympathies.

Not so with remoter disasters. Over the slaughter of Armenians by Turks she had once sobbed bitterly, and even over the devastation of the Japanese by earthquake she had mourned a little; because, though she had never known Armenians or Japanese, she had thought somewhat about them; though they had never approached her person, they had penetrated her intellect a little. But Negroes she had always accepted with horses, mules and motors, and though they had brushed her shoulder, they had never actually entered her head.

But now something had occurred to her.

'Linda you're quite different from most, er—coloured people, aren't you?'

To Linda, who had no idea what 'most coloured people' might mean, this was a baffling question. 'I don't know, Miss Cramp,' she said.

'I mean, you know, you're—I hadn't noticed before. You're really quite pretty.' She was experiencing the difficulties familiar to all who itch with curiosity but prefer not to be seen scratching. 'You're so light, you know.'

Linda's lips twitched. 'Why, I'm not so awfully light, Miss Cramp. And plenty folks lighter than I am are far from being pretty.'

'Yes—of course,' Miss Cramp considered. 'Even white people. To be sure. But of course you meant—er—coloured. But your hair now—it isn't kinky.' At once an assertion and a question.

The only answer was: 'No, Miss Cramp.'

'And how can you afford to wear such nice-looking things on eighteen dollars a week?'

'Well,' Linda said, ''course I could do better on twenty.'

Miss Cramp did not hear this, but observed, 'Patent-leather pumps and a black satin dress—'

'They're cheap shoes,' Linda explained. 'Just look nice 'cause they're new. The dress I got down on Eighth Avenue for seven dollars.'

'But your skin, my dear. You might pass for a Sicilian or an Armenian.'

Linda was not sure about these. 'I was a gypsy once in a concert,' she admitted.

'A concert?'

'At church.'

'You go to church?'

'I like to go very much.'

'Now that's just what I wanted to ask you about. Your people are very religious creatures, aren't they?'

'Well, some are and some not.'

'I thought—er—slavery, you know, would have made you very religious.'

'Maybe it did,' said Linda. 'I wouldn't know about that.'

'But don't you have your own hymns? Spirituals, I believe they are called.'

'Not in my church,' Linda said.

'What church is that, Linda?'

'Saint Augustine's,' said Linda. 'It's Episcopal.'

'Episcopal!' incredulously. 'Why, *I'm* an Episcopalian.' The tone indicated clearly that there must be some mistake.

A little devilishly, Linda smiled, but all she said was: 'Is that so?'

'But you—' began Miss Cramp, then reconsidered. 'But you must sing spirituals. All Negroes sing spirituals, don't they?'

Doubtfully Linda ruminated. 'Why—I remember some jubilee singers gave a concert of them once at the Parish. And I've been to Methodist revival meetings where they sang 'em just like jazz. We only went for fun, to see the folks get happy and shout. I've never heard them at my church in regular service, though.'

'Well,' said Miss Cramp. And again, 'Well.' Then, 'What I was getting at was—do your churches make any effort to improve conditions, to render any real service to your people?'

'Oh, yes. We have an employment agency. They sent me to the one that sent me to you.'

'No, no, Linda.' So stupid a reply restored Miss Cramp's self-assurance. 'That is not what I mean, my dear. I mean the people that are mentally ill, the criminals, the dope-fiends, the fallen women. Do your churches try to help them?'

'I don't think so—not unless they're members.'

'There must be some organization to do such work among your people,' Miss Cramp insisted.

'Well,' Linda suggested brightly, 'maybe the same organization does it that does it among your people.'

'Of course, of course. One would think so, wouldn't one?

But I haven't come in contact with—of course, I haven't worked in coloured communities—'

After a vacuous pause, Linda said: 'Maybe you mean the G.I.A.'

'G.I.A.? What's that?'

'General Improvement Association.'

'What do they do?'

'Well, they collect a dollar a year from everybody that joins, and whenever there's a lynching down south they take the dollar and send somebody to go look at it.'

'Whatever's the good of that?'

'I don't know, Miss Cramp. Seems like they just want to make sure it really happened.'

'Well. Then what do they do?'

'Well, by that time the year's up and it's time to collect another dollar. So they collect it.'

'Why don't they turn their attentions to conditions here at home?' Miss Agatha wanted to know. 'There must be much to be done here among you—an alien, primitive people in a great, strange metropolis. Why don't they do something here?'

'Well, nobody gets lynched here.'

The simplicity of this response did not satisfy Miss Cramp, who could never have suspected that her coloured maid would dare make game of her ignorance or play upon her credulity.

'Why, I can't understand—I really can't. Here is a situation that surely needs attention, and the people do nothing, absolutely nothing, about it. Lynchings—of all things! When right here in New York City there are—how many of you are there here, Linda?'

'Two hundred thousand, according to Father Bruce.'

'Oh, that's an exaggeration, of course. But even if there are as many as ten thousand, a great work could be done among them. This organization you mention—'

'The G.I.A.'

'Yes—quite evidently needs someone to point the way. Therr' attention is entirely in the wrong quarter.'

'Why didn't you help them out, Miss Cramp?'

'That's just what occurred to me, Linda. Exactly what occurred to me. When I saw you this morning and noticed for the first time how different you were from most coloured people, I said to myself, "There now—why can't they all be like that?" And I said, "Why, they *can* be if they have the right sort of help. Some organization that could render real service, that's just what they need!" Then you mentioned this G.A.R.—'

'G.I.A.'

'—And told me of the mistake they were making, and I said, "There now, there is an instrument that can be turned to good use in the proper hands." Yes indeed, Linda, I think I *will* help them out. I really do think I will.'

'They'll certainly appreciate it, Miss Cramp.'

'Of course . . . Well, that's all, Linda. Thank you very much. Linda, bring me the 'phone book when you come back, won't you? I presume they have a telephone?'

'Who, Miss Cramp?'

'This G.I.R. Society.'

'A telephone? I don't know, Miss Cramp.' Linda was elaborately uncertain, eventually concluding: 'They might have one. They might at that. I'll bring the book, Miss Cramp.'

CHAPTER VII

THERE is at least one occasion a year when Manhattan Casino requires no decorations—the occasion of the General Improvement Association's Annual Costume Ball. The guests themselves are all the decoration that is necessary.

This is not only because many guests attend in costume, but also because, of all the crowds which Manhattan Casino holds during the year, none presents a greater inherent variety. There is variety of personal station that extends from the rattiest rat to the dicktiest dickty, for this is not an exclusive, invitational 'function' but a widely advertised public affair and it is supported by everybody, because the proceeds are to be given over to Negro advancement. There is variety of personal appearance that ranges from the dingiest dinge to the most delicate pink; variety of age, from little brown gnomes of nine or ten to Cleopatras of sixty; variety, finally, of occupation, related of course to variety of social standing. At the So-and-So's Dance you would find chiefly doctors, lawyers and undertakers; at the Speedway Club Dance, bootleggers, big-time gamblers, professional politicians; at the Barbers' Ball, barbers, chauffeurs and head-waiters. Anybody may achieve admittance to any one of these, but the crowd somehow remains in large measure distinct and characteristic. Not so with the G.I.A. Costume Ball. This is the one occasion in Harlem when everybody is present and nobody minds. The bootleggers raise no objection to their rivals, the doctors. The K.M.s are seldom, if ever, seen to turn up their noses at the school teachers. Elevator boys and gamblers together discuss their ups and downs: and the richest real estate man in the colony greets his bootblack with a cordial smile. The bars are down. This is for the Race. One great common fellowship in one great common cause.

There was the great dance floor, large as a city block, with a fifteen-piece orchestra exhausting itself at the far end. On either side of this dance area, separated from it by railings and extending the length of the building between the dance floor and the lateral walls, a raised level or low terrace, occupied by a tangle of round-top tables and wire-legged chairs. Either terrace broken midway by a wide staircase that turned at right angles and led up alongside the wall to the upper level, the level of the tier of boxes that encircled the hall and roofed in the two lateral terraces below.

Those who between dances repaired only so far as the terraces and sat at the round-top tables and drank Whistle, perhaps tinctured with corn, were either just ordinary respectable people or rats. But those who mounted the stairs and crowded into or about the boxes, who kept waiters busy bringing ginger ale, which they flavoured from silver hip flasks—those were dickties and fays.

Of the people downstairs, a few of the girls wore inexpensive costumes; others wore gaudy habiliments that were just as truly costumes but were probably not so intended. The men wore anything, from clothing so inconspicuous as to attract no attention to outfits positively stunning—light grey suits, cerise crêpe ties and bright yellow, broad-toed oxfords.

Of the dickties, the women were all extravagantly dressed. Whether they wore costume or evening frock, it quite obviously had to outglitter everyone else's. The men, however, uniformly clad in dinner-coats, performed well their sole aesthetic function of background.

Of the usual sprinkling of fays, a few were the friends and guests of dickties; several were members of the Executive Board of the G.I.A., professional uplifters, determined to be broad-minded about this thing; and accompanying these two groups, a third consisting of newcomers to Harlem—all gasps, grunts and ill-concealed squirms, or sighs and astonished smiles. The first group coming to enjoy not the Negroes but themselves, hence perfectly at ease; the second coming to raise up the darker brother, hence sweetly beaming and benevolent; the third coming to see the niggers, hence tortured with smothered comment and stifled expression. On the whole corresponding pretty well to their hosts, these visitors: usually dull and ordinary, occasionally bright and substantial, once in a blue moon brilliant or beautiful.

So swept the scene from black to white through all the shadows and shades. Ordinary Negroes and rats below, dickties and fays above, the floor beneath the feet of the one constituting the roof over the heads of the other. Somehow, undeniably, a predominance of darker skins below, and, just as undeniably, of fairer skins above. Between them, stairways to climb. One might have read in that distribution a complete philosophy of skin-colour, and from it deduced the past, present and future of these people . . . Out on the dance floor, everyone, dickty and rat, rubbed joyous elbows, laughing, mingling, forgetting differences. But whenever the music stopped everyone immediately sought his own level.

One great common fellowship in one great common cause.

CHAPTER VIII

DOWNSTAIRS at one point on the terrace were Jinx and Bubber, oblivious to everybody, arguing heatedly over the relative speed of corn and gin as intoxicants. Neither had either. At another point, a group of girls dressed as gypsies sat laughing around a table. The prettiest of these was Linda, not the dry and quiet Linda that served Agatha Cramp her meals, but a vivacious light-hearted child, out on a lark, being herself. Not far away, leaning against one of the pillars that supported the tier of boxes, stood Henry Patmore, calculatingly watching Linda. Further back, unnoticed, like a great shadow against the wall, Shine stood with his hands in his pockets, motionless, watching Patmore.

He had not long to wait before what he anticipated began to happen.

Henry Patmore was acknowledged among his friends as a perfect ladies' man. He had all the qualifications: money to burn, with a constant large supply of bank notes on his person, after the fashion of bootleggers; excellent taste in dress, as exemplified tonight by a sack suit of light greenish grey, a shirt of slate radium silk with collar to match, a bright green satin cravat caressing a diamond question mark, and a breast-pocket polka dot handkerchief, whose crêpe border matched the tie. He was large and self-assured with an engaging manner and a flashing smile. Some people might not have cared for the fishy blankness of Patmore's grey eyes, nor for his tough-looking tan skin, thickly bespecked with small brown freckles, nor for his rather heavy jowls nor his rather thick neck with its two deep transverse creases behind. But so courteous was his manner with ladies, so deferential, so flatteringly humble his approach, that almost never did a girl deny his request for a dance, whether she knew him or not.

Further, there was about him the reassuring deliberateness of complete self-confidence. He was thirty-five years old, as free of the uncertainties of youth as of the infirmities of age, on the one hand debonair but not dashing, on the other, solid but not set. He had reached a point where his person might still inspire admiration while his maturity dismissed apprehension. Never did Patmore's manner suggest his motive.

It follows that Patmore's conquests were many and his reputation enviable. Nor can it be denied that he made the most of this reputation among his fellow men, taking little pains to conceal either the nature of his activities or the identity of their object. He even allowed it to be suspected that there were dickty homes where he made it convenient to deliver liquor only during the hours when the head of the house was absent. Of this he did not openly boast, of course—not, at least, when he was sober. That would have been bad business indeed, just as it would be bad business tonight to mount the stairs and try to mingle with his many patrons in the boxes. Occasionally, however, his own liquor did make him excessively talkative. He would stride into his establishment proclaiming his own excellence in this or that particular, and not infrequently the particular was conquest of ordinarily inaccessible women. Accordingly his fellows declared him to be a 'jiver from way back'. And while, drunk or sober, he did not deny this, still he always insisted that he was business man first of all.

For today, however, his business was done. He had provided more of the life of this party than any other single person, and he now fell back with a clear conscience upon the pursuit of his avocation.

As a field for such an avocation, the uniqueness of Harlem is that there are always new realms to conquer. Incredible, bewildering variety. Consider the mere item of complexion, you whose choice may run only from cool white to warm rose-and-olive. Harlem offers its cool white too, with blue eyes and flaxen hair, believe it or not; proceeds on through the conventional shades to the warmth of rose-and-olive; and here, where the rest of Manhattan ends, Harlem has just begun: on through the creams, the honeys and high-browns, the browns, the sealskins and chestnuts—a dozen gradations in every class, not one without its peculiar richness. And if white be cool and olive warm, must not chestnut be downright fever? Harlemites swear that the Queen of Sheba was without doubt a sealskin brown and further insist that Cleopatra could have been but a honey at the fairest. And for evidence they will point out a dozen Shebas and any number of Cleopatras in the flesh.

Here is every variation of skin-colour, every variety of feature-form, every possible combination of these variations and varieties. And of course every imaginable result, from the most outrageous ugliness to the most extraordinary beauty. Harlem is superlatively rich in diversity.

Accordingly, Henry Patmore enjoyed almost boundless choice, and it was no mean tribute to Linda's beauty that tonight his wandering eye fell and lingered upon her. He saw that she was with other girls and therefore probably unattended—legit-imate prey. And if he caught something vaguely different about her, it but served to heighten his interest.

Shine too had seen Linda and recognized her as the girl of the Court Avenue comments. It had given him strange and moving sensations, this recognition—had made him stare again just as foolishly as he had stared that morning a fortnight before. For him, the rest of the picture thereupon faded into back-ground, grew abruptly distant—people, laughter, shouting, music—while this dark-eyed girl in her gypsy attire, scarlet, gold and black, became and remained the centre and reason of it all.

Joshua Jones, be it confessed, was himself a person of impor-tance among the ladies. There had been girls aplenty: Sarah Mosely, Babe Merrimac, Lottie Buttsby, Becky Katz, Maggie Mulligan and others. An acknowledged master of men is usually attractive to women, and in his world of sinew and steel Shine had the necessary reputation; there was no end of stories about what he could do with his hands.

But his general philosophy of conduct, of being impenetrably hard, of repudiating sentiment and relaxing toward no one and nothing, shielded his spirit if not his body from the women he so far had known, and while he might have claimed some excellence as a man of affairs if he had so chosen, it would not have been the same in degree or kind as that attributed to Patmore. Patmore's victories had been achieved, Shine's had been thrust upon him, and what the one would have eagerly pursued the other intentionally eluded.

'Women,' Shine had often said, 'don't mean a man no good. Always want sump'm. Always got they hands out. Gimme. Any bird that really falls for a sheba is one half sap and th' other half sucker.'

It did not matter that he had derived this conclusion from observation rather than experience. He believed it firmly. And so it was that triumph to Patmore would have been defeat to Shine, and the former's reputation was to the latter nothing at all to brag about. Indeed, this reputation of Pat's was one of the things about him that Shine most disliked. It summed Pat up as less of a man to be so much of a sap.

A new dance began, and from the orchestra, keyed up now to its very low-downest, there issued a current of leisurely, compelling rhythm, a rising tide of rhythm which floated couple after couple off the bank into midstream. Presently Linda was left alone at her table.

Henry Patmore went forward. To request the dance, less accomplished beaus would have simply extended a hand toward the girl, an audacious gesture, bordering on the presumptuous. Not Patmore. In addition to the slightly extended hand, he bent forward in a most ingratiating bow, smiled the metallic smile which revealed so much of his wealth, and said earnestly:

'Would you do me the favour, miss?'

Linda, however, knew how to dismiss strangers. She looked up, smiled very, very sweetly, and said with great finality, 'No, thanks.'

The average sheik would have passed on. Patmore was not the average sheik; and perhaps Linda had smiled a little too sweetly to convey sarcasm. Said he:

'The next one, maybe?'

'I'm leaving after this one,' the girl lied easily.

'My, my. What a shame, both of us wastin' it.'

He drew up a chair and sat down, his manner indicating clearly that though she might not dance with him, she could have no objection to his sharing her table. And he casually continued the conversation.

'You got a good chance to win the costume prize,' he observed.

Linda, silently annoyed, was on the point of rising to leave. His next remark detained her:

'I'm one o' the judges, you know.'

Her brows went up and he knew that now, at least, he had her interest. It quickened his own. A girl who was wise would have answered, 'Yea—and I'm Norma Talmadge.'

Linda, instead, exclaimed without irony, 'Are they really going to give prizes?'

Patmore grinned within, congratulating himself on his own good fortune. 'Ripe in the body and green in the head. What more could a man want?'

'No lie,' he assured her. 'And I'm go'n' vote for you—unanimous.'

Of course, if you happened to be wearing a costume and unexpectedly found a prize in sight, there was no sense in throwing a chance away. And if this courteous man was a judge, that meant he must be Somebody and not just an ordinary masher as she had supposed.

'I been noticin' you specially,' he said.

She was decently silent.

'That's why I asked you to dance. Wanted to find out all about you.' He took out his business address-book, which contained the names and addresses of many prominent Harlemites, and wrote the words which he repeated after her aloud:

'"Miss Linda Young. Three hundred and nine Court Avenue, Washington Heights." Fine. Fine. Miss Young, the first prize is twenty-five dollars, and it's as good as yours right now.'

'Oh, no—'

'"Deed so. Now listen, Miss Young. My name is Patmore— Henry Patmore—and we might just as well be friends. And if you'll finish this dance with me, I'll see that the other judges get a good look at you.'

Shine, several yards away, could hear nothing that was said, but he saw the whole thing: first, the girl's obvious reaction to being approached by a stranger; despite this, the ease with which she had been engaged in conversation; then the promptness with which she had given over her name and address to be written in the new friend's notebook. Now he saw her smile and rise and let Patmore steer her to the dance floor. In a moment more the pair was engulfed in the stream.

The scene occasioned in Shine a curious reaction: not an intensification of his contempt for Patmore, as might have been expected, but an unaccountably violent revulsion of feeling toward the girl. His inordinate admiration turned to equally inordinate scorn.

'As easy as that!' he scowled. 'Well, I be damned!'

CHAPTER IX

OF COURSE he now fell back on his own unfailing gospel.

'See?' said he to the cock-eyed world, 'that jes' goes to show you, see? One more sheba, that's all; More different they look, less different they are. Bet he offered her a stick of candy or something . . . And here I come near getting excited just looking at her. Can you beat it?'

But though this might be only one more instance of a far-reaching general truth, somehow the cynic did not dismiss it with customary casualness. As the evening progressed, he admitted this to himself, indeed could not deny it. For even after he had danced through 'Do it, Daddy,' with Babe Merrimac, who vamped him desperately without avail, and through a slow and easy, somewhat disturbing 'Shake That Thing' with the voluptuous Lottie Buttsby, the earlier incident still stuck fast in his mind. Babe and Lottie both complained of finding him even less enthusiastic than usual. He was, they avowed, downright leaden, and Lottie specified precisely where anyone interested could find the lead. But neither succeeded in bantering him into promising to see her safely home after the shout.

He caught sight of Linda occasionally, dancing with boys. Nice, Sunday-Schoolish boys he did not know, and he blamed these occasional views of her for the persistence in his mind of what he had seen. He began to resent that persistence:

'What the hell I keep thinking 'bout *that* for?'

Then, by way of excuse, 'Well she sure is good to look at. Ain't no sense in a woman bein' that good-lookin'. Ain't no excuse for it. Dangerous, what I mean. Ought to be locked up somewhere where she couldn't do so much harm.'

* * *

50

He encountered Jinx and Bubber and they did nothing to help him forget.

'Boy!' exclaimed Bubber, 'remember that sheba we seen that mornin' on Court Avenue?'

Shine grunted assent.

'She's right here at d'belly-rub tonight, big boy. Sharp out this world. We jes' seen her—right over yonder. Great Gordon Gin—talk about one red hot mamma! Dressed like a fortune-teller—wish she'd tell mine. Anything she say 'd be all right with me. Tell me I go'n' to die tomorrow, I'd go right on and die happy.'

'I *mean*,' Jinx agreed. 'And when I was dead and buried, all she'd have to do would be walk over my grave, see? And damn if I wouldn't get up and follow her. Boy, she's got what it takes, and papa don't mean maybe!'

'She's the owl's bow'ls,' Bubber epitomised.

Shine looked at them scornfully. 'You guys,' he observed, 'must both have glass eyes.'

When he had glumly departed, they looked at each other a long time solemnly; then they grinned and finally laughed aloud.

'What's a matter with my boy?' Jinx wanted to know.

'Nothin'. She jes' done put the locks on 'im, that's all.'

'Nothin' different. And then up and give him lots of air.'

'Seems like,' Bubber grew serious, 'our boy has been smote sure enough, though, don't it?'

'Smit,' corrected Jinx.

'Smote.'

'Smit.'

'What you know 'bout language?'

'More 'n you. Don't nobody talk language down in yo' home in South Carolina.'

'What they talk, then?'

'Don't talk at all. Jes' grunt.'

'Yea—and so did that man grunt what run you out o' Virginia, too.'

'That's all right 'bout that. Fact is, every time you forget you up north, you start gruntin' in yo' native language.'

'Maybe. But what I mean, you don't never *forget* you up north—and ain't nobody never heard you sing that song 'bout "Carry Me Back to Old Virginny" neither.'

'The word is smit.'

'Smote.'

'Smit, I say.'

'Listen, squirrel-fodder. When you get a letter in yo' mail what somebody *write* you, it's *wrote*, ain't it?'

'You listen, Oscar. When you get a hole in yo' hiney where some dog *bite* you, you *bit*, ain't you?'

The debate between these two was no more undecided than another, conducted within the mind of Joshua Jones. The question at issue was this: If Henry Patmore had so easily picked up the girl, why should not he pick her up also? Or—why should he?

On the one side were all the customary objections of his avowed attitude toward women. On the other were a number of obscure things, imponderable as vapour, but just as present and annoying: an impulse to win her favour just to have the pleasure of discarding it, compensating somewhat thus for his own recent disillusion; a plaguing curiosity to observe the girl at close range and satisfy the suspicion that she couldn't be all that she seemed to be at a distance; a thought of riling Patmore by outdoing him at his own game and robbing him of this, his latest triumph; these but the half-conscious excuses, really, for a far simpler, unadmitted urge: the unquestionably compelling attractiveness of the girl herself.

This debate terminated suddenly and decisively. Linda finished a dance with one of the Sunday School boys, and now, completely bored, shooed him off into the crowd, insisting that otherwise the following dance would begin before he could find his next partner. She came now unaccompanied toward the low terrace, reaching it just as the orchestra struck up a new number. Here she and Shine met face to face and the argument was settled. She was alone, she was at hand, and a new dance was beginning.

Their eyes met and he grinned and said:

'Didn't you promise me this one?'

It. was a good grin, wide, honest-looking, a trifle amused, a trifle audacious. His chin assumed more than its usual challenge, and the flash of his teeth set up twinkling echoes in his eyes. It was a perfectly spontaneous, disarming grin and it ought to have turned the trick. But it failed.

The girl looked at him a moment at first surprised, then puzzled; then, with a little smile of comprehension and disdain, brushed past him without a word.

The superiority of that smile was far and away more telling and convincing than any scornful toss of the head or sneer or gesture of anger could have been. It placed the notion of dancing with him beyond anger, resentment or contempt. It stamped such a possibility as too absurd to be aught but a trifle amusing. And it raised Shine's temperature.

On the impulse of his anger he turned and followed her the short distance to her table, and when she sat down and looked up, there he was. She was mildly astonished.

'Wrong number,' she said briefly and smiled that smile again.

He sat down and put his arms on the table and leaned forward as she drew back in surprise. He spoke very gravely, and his voice, though low, suffered no loss of clarity by reason of the bedlam around about; indeed the merry confusion seemed to lend them a certain seclusion.

'Listen, Long Distance—who you kiddin'?'

'Wrong number, I said,' the girl repeated less generously and pushed back her chair to rise.

'One moment please, operator,' returned Shine. 'What number did you think I was callin'?'

'The number on that policeman's badge,' she said, although 'that policeman' was nowhere in sight.

'Where?' He looked about unconcernedly.

'Or—one of the officials.'

'Officials?'

'Yes, officials!'

'Oh. They all friends o' mine.'

'Mr Henry Patmore, I suppose?'

'Who?'

'Henry Patmore.' She knew that would settle him.

'Pat . . . ? Well I take it back. I know him well but he ain't no friend o' mine.'

There was but one way to keep him from imperturbably trailing her the rest of the evening: she had recourse to insult:

'No—he wouldn't be.'

That went wide. 'What official is he—official bootlegger?'

'He's a judge—and a gentleman.'

'Judge? Judge of what?'

'Of costumes—and of people that try to be sheiks.'

He looked at her as she sat on the edge of the chair, a bird poised, postponing flight only for one last jab at the snake; and instead of laughing aloud at what she had said about Patmore, he scowled and muttered, 'Judge. Humph. So that was his jive. Huh. Judge.'

This piqued her curiosity and further delayed her departure. 'Yes, judge.'

'What else did he tell you?'

'Nothing else about himself—but a whole lot about you.'

'Me?'

'Yes, you.'

'Me? How he come to—?'

'I saw you looking and asked him.' She rose at last. 'I promised him this dance, if'—no missing the sarcasm this time—'if you will excuse me.'

'No—wait a minute, listen.' He too was standing now, towering over her, leaning a trifle toward her, and perhaps less composed than he'd ever been in his life in the company of a girl. If she had been interested enough to ask Pat about him, there was no sense in releasing her now so easily, just because she was playing tight. Or maybe she wasn't playing. Maybe she was scared. 'Listen—I admit I got you all wrong. But it looked . . . Listen. I'm standing over there, see? And Pat comes up and puts on his jive—anybody can see you don't know him. But you lap it up. You swallow it whole. I mean that's the way it looked. Naturally I figure I can get away too, see? You can't kill me for that, can you?'

From Shine this was abject apology. Babe would have taken it so, or Lottie, and been delighted and amazed. But Linda, to whom his implication was insult, stiffened as if something unclean had touched her, while her eyes dilated with anger and resentment. Then her body relaxed into an attitude of casual contempt and her look became tranquil scorn. She said quietly, as if verifying a memory:

'Mr Patmore said you were just a dirty rat.'

At first the words merely stuck in his ears unrealized and meaningless, like the monotonous pulse of the orchestra's bass drum. Then suddenly, as if their beating had finally broken through a wall, they burst full into consciousness and throbbed in his head like pain.

He stood quite still, experiencing new and terrible feelings. Rat. Well enough from an equal—but from this girl . . . Rat. Dirty rat. Patmore *said* you were just a dirty rat.

Linda saw the change come over his face; saw the brows contract, the eyes gleam, the jaws tighten, the lips set; saw his body go taut like a rope under tension and the bronze skin lose its life and turn dirty copper. Linda had not the sophistication nor the cultivated self-protective cruelty of most beautiful women. She did not see that she had achieved her purpose, had effected a serious wound, and could now perhaps go on her way unafraid. She saw only that her thrust had gone too deep and said impulsively:

'Oh, I'm sorry—I didn't really mean that—'

Then, in a flutter of contrition and fright she whirled about and fled.

For yet a while longer he did not move. Music, dancing, laughter—tumultuous silence, uproarious, crowded solitude. Presently he was aware of a voice periodically snarling 'R-r-rat!' and after a while realized that the trap-drummer was executing a series of rolls, each swelling to a terminal snap like the epithet. 'R-r-rat!'

That woke him. The stupor had been the recession of a wave, withdrawing only to gather new impetus. Now again it rushed over him, hot and impelling. He looked about a little madly and very grimly, and he said aloud:

'Judge. Hmph. Show me that judge. I'm go'n' give 'im sump'm to judge.'

CHAPTER X

UPSTAIRS in the box of J. Pennington Potter, who was one of the dozen vice-presidents of the General Improvement Association, an incredibly ill-chosen variety of personalities squirmed. It was J. Pennington Potter's conviction that only admixture produced harmony between races. He argued quite logically. Prejudice and misunderstanding were due to mutual ignorance and ignorance due to silence. This silence must be broken. How break it save by acquaintanceship—how acquaint save by admixture? Social admixture—there was the solution to all the problems of race.

And so he proceeded to admix. There was himself, proud, loud and pompous, and his wife, round, brown and expansive, who always seemed bursting with something to say, but had never been known to say it, a woman so inflated with her husband's bombast that one felt she'd collapse at a single thrust. There was the Hon. Buckram Byle, an ex-alderman from the twenty-ninth district, whose presence was intended to give the party some notion of the dignity of a Negro public servant. This he assuredly did, his habit being to stand apart, alone, with folded arms, motionless, silent, scowling, in the deeps of meditation. But few suspected the real basis of this air: that Mr Byle was simply very angry at his young and pretty wife, Nora, who had managed to elude his jealously watchful eye all evening, and that the scowl, as usual, evidenced his resolution to take her straight home the moment she should reappear. There was Noel Dunn, the Nordic editor of an anti-Nordic journal, who missed no item of scene or conversation that he thought he could use for copy. Dunn's readers gobbled up pro-Negro pieces, not because they were pro-Negro so much as because they were anti-White, and he and Mrs Dunn were frequent visitors to Harlem, finding the Pennington Potters convenient wedges in effecting several profitable entrances.

The Potters were very proud of this friendship, and J. Pennington never missed a chance to mention, parentheticaly of course, that Mr and Mrs Noel Dunn were up to dinner the night before last. The Dunns were known among their friends to mention these excursions also, but not at all parenthetically. The Dunns always explained elaborately about the 'wealth of material' to be found in Negro Harlem, and they punctuated their apologies with different intonations of the word 'marvellous'. Everything in Harlem, to the Dunns, was simply 'marvellous!'

A friend of the Dunns, one Tony Nayle, who was visiting Harlem for the first time, was absent from the box at the moment. He had found the music and Nora Byle an irresistible combination; and Nora admitted later that she had continued dancing with him not merely to aggravate her jealous spouse, but also to verify what at first she could hardly believe. Nora always insisted that fays danced with a rhythm all their own, if any. She found Tony Nayle to be the first fay partner she'd ever known, so she said, to dance as though he was paying any attention to the music at all.

And finally, side by side in the front of the box, sat Fred Merrit and Miss Agatha Cramp.

It would have been enough to kill the spirit of any party just to have the inarticulate Mrs Potter as its hostess; enough to distress any company just to inject into it a chronically jealous husband like Byle, let alone bringing his pretty wife, Nora, into contact with the attractive and willing-to-learn Tony; enough to insure discomfort in any group to include guests whose purposes were so different—amusement, profit, uplift; difficult enough to bring together unacquainted, dissimilar people without attempting to mix diverse motives as well. But to have put Fred Merrit and Miss Agatha Cramp side by side—this was the master touch; only a J. Pennington Potter could have done that.

* * *

One view only did they all have in common, the scene on the floor below.

'Marvellous!' said Mr Dunn.

'Marvellous!' echoed Mrs Dunn.

'Wonderful!' said J. Pennington Potter with a certain air of discovery.

So dense was the crowd of dancers, so close each couple to the next, that an observer from above might easily have lost the sense that these were actually people. They seemed rather some turbulent congress of bright coloured, inanimate things, propelled by a force over which they had no control. The couples were like the leaves and petals of flowers strewn thick on a stream; describing little individual figures and turns, circling capriciously in groups here and there, but all borne steadily onward in one common undertrend. Each seemed to answer with a smile the whim of every breeze; all actually obeyed unaware the steadfast pull of the current.

'Marvellous!' echoed the Dunns.

'Wonderful!' said J. Pennington Potter.

'M-m—' grunted the Hon. Buckram Byle.

'Don't you think, Penny,' said Noel Dunn, 'that your organization would be more specifically defined if it were named The General Negro Improvement Association?'

'Why, yes. Yes indeed. That is, perhaps. As a matter of fact we originally conceived the name as the General Negro Improvement Association. But it was I myself who contended, and without successful contradiction, that any improvement of the American Negro would inevitably improve all other Americans as well. There was therefore—ah—no point, you see, in including the word "Negro", and I succeeded in having it deleted.'

Mr Dunn smiled, noting that the trap-drummer was at the moment very amusing.

* * *

Meanwhile Miss Agatha Cramp sat quite overwhelmed at the strangeness of her situation. This was her introduction to the people she planned to uplift. True to her word she had personally investigated the G.I.A. and been welcomed with open arms. Certain members of the executive board knew her and her past works—one or two had been associated with her in other projects—and her experience, resources and devotion to service were unanimously acclaimed assets. And nobody minded her excessively corrective attitude—all new board members started out revising things. Furthermore, the Costume Ball was at hand and that would be enough to upset anybody's ideas of revision.

Never had Miss Cramp seen so many Negroes in one place at one time. Moreover, never had she dreamed that so many of her own people would for any reason imaginable have descended to mingle with these Negroes. She had prided herself on her own liberality in joining this company tonight. And so it shocked and outraged her to see that most of these fair-skinned visitors were unmistakably enjoying themselves, instead of maintaining the aloof, kindly dignity proper to those who must sacrifice to serve. And of course little did she suspect how many of the fair-skinned ones were not visitors at all but natives.

When she met Nora Byle, for instance, she was first struck with the beauty of her 'Latin type'. To save her soul she could not help a momentary stiffening when Buckram Byle, who was a jaundice-brown, was presented as Nora's husband. Intermarriage! She recovered. No. The girl was one of those mulattos, of course, a conclusion that brought but temporary relief, for the next moment the debonair Tony Nayle had gone off with the 'mulatto', both of them flirting disgracefully.

It was all in all a situation which robbed Miss Cramp of words, but she smiled bravely through her distress and found no little relief in sitting beside Fred Merrit, whose perfect manner, cherubic smile and fair skin were highly comforting. She had not yet noticed the significant texture of his hair.

'Well, what do you think of it?' Merrit eventually asked.

'I don't know what to think, really. What do you think?'

'I? Why—it's all too familiar now for me to have thoughts about. I take it for granted.'

'Oh—you have worked among Negroes a great deal, then?'

Merrit grinned. 'All my life.'

'How do you find them?'

That Merrit did not resist temptation and admit his complete identity at this point is easier to explain than to excuse. There was first his admitted joy in discomfiting members of the dominant race. Further, however, there was a special complex of reasons closer at hand.

Merrit was far more outraged by the flirtation between Nora Byle and Tony Nayle than had been even Miss Cramp herself, and with greater cause. His own race prejudice was a bitterer, more deep-seated emotion than was hers, and out of it came an attitude that caused him to look with great suspicion and distrust upon all visitors who came to Harlem 'socially'. He insisted that the least blameworthy motive that brought them was curiosity, and held that he, for one, was not on exhibition. As for the men who came oftener than once, he felt that they all had but one motive, the pursuit of Harlem women; that their cultivation of Harlem men was a blind and an instrument in achieving this end, and that the end itself was always illicit and therefore reprehensible.

It was with him a terribly serious matter, of which he could see but one side. When Langdon once hinted gently that maybe it was a two-way reaction, he snorted the suggestion away as nonsense. That he should allow it to disturb him so profoundly meant that it went profoundly back into his own life, as it did into the lives of most people of heredity so diverse as his. The everyday difficulty of his own adjustment engendered in him an unforgiving hatred of those past generations responsible for it. Hence every suggestion that history might repeat itself in this particular occasioned revolt. If there could be no fair exchange, said he, let there be no exchange at all.

He knew that no two ardent individuals would ever be concerned with any such formulas, but the very ineffectuality of what seemed to him so just a principle rendered its violation the more irritating. And in the particular case of Tony and Nora—well, he rather liked Nora himself.

And so beneath his pleasant manner, there was a disordered spirit which at this moment almost gleefully accepted the chance to vent itself on Miss Agatha Cramp's ignorance. To admit his identity would have wholly lost him this chance. And as for the fact that she was a woman, that only made the compensation all the more complete, gave it a quality of actual retaliation, of parallel all the more satisfying.

'How do I find Negroes? I like them very much. Ever so much better than white people.'

'Oh Mr Merrit! Really?'

'You see, they have so much more colour.'

'Yes. I can see that.' She gazed upon the mob. 'How primitive these people are,' she murmured. 'So primeval. So unspoiled by civilization.'

'Beautiful savages,' suggested Merrit.

'Exactly. Just what I was thinking. What abandonment—what unrestraint—'

'Almost as bad as a Yale-Harvard football game, isn't it?' Merrit's eyes twinkled.

'Well,' Miss Cramp demurred, 'that's really quite a different thing, you know.'

'Of course. This unrestraint is the kind that is hostile to society, hostile to civilization. This is the sort of thing that you and I as sociologists must contend with, must wipe out.'

'Yes indeed. Quite so. This sort of thing is, as you say, quite unfortunate. We must educate these people out of it. There is so much to be done.'

'Listen to that music. Savage too, don't you think?'

'Just what had occurred to me. That music is like the beating of—what do they call 'em? Dum-dums, isn't it?'

'I was just trying to think what it recalled,' mused Merrit with great seriousness. 'Tom-toms! That's it—of course. How stupid of me. Tom-toms. And the shuffle of feet—'

'Rain,' breathed Miss Cramp, who, since her new interest, had deemed it her duty to read some of Langdon's poetry. 'Rain falling in a jungle.'

'Rain?'

'Rain falling on banana leaves,' said the lady. And the gentleman assented:

'I know how it is. I once fell on a banana peel myself.'

'So primitive.' Miss Cramp turned to Mrs Dunn, who sat behind and above her. 'The throb of the jungle,' she remarked.

'Marvellous!' exhaled Mrs Dunn.

'These people—we can do so much for them—we must educate them out of such unrestraint.'

Whereupon Tony and Nora appeared laughing and breathless at the box entrance; and Tony, descendant of Cedrics and Caesars, loudly declared:

'I'm going to get that bump-the-bump dance if it takes me the whole darn night!'

'Bump the what?' Miss Agatha wondered.

'Come on, Gloria,' Tony urged Mrs Dunn. 'You ought to know it, long as you've, been coming to Harlem. Mrs Byle gives me up. You try.'

Mrs Dunn smiled and quickly rose. 'I'll say I will. Come along. It's perfectly marvellous.'

'Furthermore,' expounded J. Pennington Potter, 'there is a tendency among Negro organizations to incorporate too many words in a single designation with the result that what is intended as mere appelation becomes a detailed description. Take for example the N.O.U.S.E. and the I.N.I.A.W. There can be no excuse for entitlements of such prolixity. They endeavour to encompass a society's past, present and future, embracing as well a description of motive and instrument. There is no call you will agree, no excuse, no justification for deline-ation, history and prophecy in a single title.'

'Quite so, Penny,' said Mr Dunn. 'Mrs Byle, may I have this dance?'

'Certainly,' said Nora, smiling a trifle too amusedly.

'We're going home after this one,' growled her husband as she passed.

Miss Cramp said in a low voice to Merrit:

'Isn't he a wonderful person?'

'Who?' wondered Merrit.

'Mr Potter. He talks so beautifully and seems so intelligent.'

'He is intelligent, isn't he?' said Merrit, as if the discovery surprised him.

'He must have an awfully good head.'

'Unexcelled for certain purposes.'

'I had no idea they were ever so cultured. How simple our task would be if they were all like that.'

'Like Potter? Heaven forbid!'

'Oh, Mr Merrit. Really you mustn't let your prejudices prevail. Negroes deserve at least a few leaders like that.'

'I don't know what they've ever done to deserve them,' he said.

Unable to win him over to her broader viewpoint, she changed the subject.

'Mrs Byle is very pretty, isn't she?'

'Yes.'

'She is so light in complexion for a Negress.'

'A what?'

'A Negress. She *is* a Negress, isn't she?'

'Well, I suppose you'd call her that.'

'It *is* hard to appreciate, isn't it? It makes one wonder, really. Mrs Byle is almost as fair as I am, while—well, look at that girl down there. Absolutely black. Yet both—'

'Are Negresses.'

'Exactly what I was thinking. I was just thinking now, how long have there been Negroes in our country, Mr Merrit?'

'Longer than most one hundred percent Americans, I believe.'

'Really?'

'Since around 1500, I understand. And in numbers since 1619.'

'How well informed you are, Mr Merrit. Imagine knowing dates like that . . . Why, that's between three and four hundred years ago, isn't it? But of course four hundred years isn't such a long time if you believe in evolution. I consider evolution very important, don't you?'

'Profoundly so.'

'But I was just thinking. These people have been out of their native element only three or four hundred years, and just see what it has done to their complexions! It's hard to believe that just three hundred years in our country has brought about such a great variety in the colour of the black race.'

'Environment is a powerful influence, Miss Cramp,' murmured Merrit.

'Yes, of course. Chiefly the climate, I should judge. Don't you think?'

Merrit blinked, then nodded gravely, 'Climate undoubtedly. Climate. Changed conditions of heat and moisture and so on.'

'Yes, exactly. Remarkable isn't it? Now just consider, Mr Merrit. The northern peoples are very fair—the Scandinavians, for example. The tropic peoples, on the other hand are very dark—often black like the Negroes in their own country. Isn't that true?'

'Undeniably.'

'Now if these very same people here tonight had originally gone to Scandinavia—three or four hundred years ago, you understand—some of them would by now be as fair as the Scandinavians! Why, they'd even have blue eyes and yellow hair!'

'No doubt about that,' Merrit agreed meditatively. 'Oh yes. They'd have them without question.'

'Just imagine!' marvelled Miss Cramp. 'A Negro with skin as fair as your own!'

'M-m. Yes. Just imagine,' said he without smiling.

CHAPTER XI

THE COMMENTS of the occupants of nearby boxes would have been illuminating to J. Pennington Potter's party—the box, for example, containing Cornelia Bond's guests. Among these were young Dr and Mrs Peter Long, Mrs Hernie Boston, Conrad White, who was a writer of stories about Negroes, and Betty Brown, his fiancée. Miss Cramp would have found their comments vulgar, unforgivable of Con and Betty, who had a way of forgetting all about the fact that they were white. J. Pennington Potter would have classed them as 'Preposterous!' Dunn would have taken notes and written an editorial on the passing of Nordic supremacy. Merrit would have chuckled inwardly with glee.

'Who's the scrawny new convert with the J. Popeyed Potters?' from the reputedly wealthy Cornelia, who was tall and regal in bearing and thoroughly, beautifully Ethiopian in appearance.

'There are two,' said Hernie. 'Which one?'

'Where's the two?' demanded Cornelia.

'One's off dancing with Nora Byle.'

'Nothing scrawny about *him*,' said Sarah Long.

'No,' agreed Cornelia, 'and nothing dumb. The way he's learning, it won't be long now—that Nora Byle is a dog.'

'Jealous!' grinned Hernie. 'After the way you extracted Jimmie Polio from her clutches?'

'Don't be a damn fool, Hernie. Wonder where Jimmy ran off to, come to think of it? Hasn't reported to headquarters for an hour. Sarah,' to Mrs Long, 'I want you and that bad-haired husband of yours over to a little stomp-down Saturday night. Consider yourselves flattered—Con and Betty'll be the only other shines present.' Her eye fell again on Miss Agatha Cramp. 'That's the homeliest woman in the world, bar none,' she avowed.

Peter Long, who was 'tight', rose and sang in a loud voice:

'Oh her face was sharp as a butcher's cleaber
But dat did not seem to grieb 'er—'

'She's looking right at you, Cornelia,' said Hernie.

'Yea,' said Cornelia, 'and I bet ten dollars she's saying "Beautiful savage" or "So primitive".'

Conrad said: 'Potter's got a sense of humour anyhow. Hooking her up with Gloria Dunn and Nora Byle. I'll bet Gloria snubbed her.'

'No, Con. You're the only fay I know that draws the colour line on other fays.'

'It's natural. Downtown I'm only passing. These,' he waved grandiloquently, 'are my people.'

'Yea—so you seem to think, the way you sell 'em for cash,' said Cornelia.

'They enjoy being sold,' returned Con.

Betty said: 'Don't you think that Nora Byle has the most beautiful hands in the world?'

'I never pay much attention to her—hands,' grinned Con.

'All the girls I know in Harlem have beautiful hands,' Betty complained.

'You don't know many, then,' Cornelia remarked.

'Just look at mine,' Betty went on. 'Pudgy as a poodle's paw. This Caucasian superiority stuff is a lot of bunk.'

'Don't let your liquor out-talk you, Betty.'

'No danger,' said Betty. Then, 'Say—do you know what I'm going to do?'

'Commit suicide,' suggested Cornelia.

'In a way. I'm going to write a novel much better than anything Con has done—'

'Not much of an ambition—'

'—and present it as the work of a Negro.'

'Negress,' corrected Hernie with irony.

'Well,' said Con, 'you can be sure of two things.'

'What?'

'You can be sure some critic will call it the best thing ever done by a Negro.'

'Yes,' said Cornelia, 'as if that's paying you a hell of a compliment.'

'And,' Con continued, 'you can be sure that some fay will insist that it should have been more African.'

'And the critic's name,' said Cornelia, 'will probably be Rabinowitch.'

A tall, very blond young man with rosy cheeks, whose eyelids were ptotic with alcohol, came clambering into the box as if he had six pairs of feet.

'Where's my Ethiopian?' he cried at the top of his lungs, peering about myopically and waving his arms like antennae. 'Hey! Where's my Ethiopian queen?'

'Jimmy!' called Cornelia. 'Bottle that racket. Come here and sit down, you imp.'

'Where?' pleaded Jimmy Polio. 'Can't see you at all, really. Can't seem to get my silly eyes open—'

'Look, Con,' said Betty, indicating Miss Agatha Cramp, who had heard Jimmy's cry and was now observing from a distance. 'Look at the horror on that poor woman's face. She's just about ready to die.'

Together they looked at the wide-eyed Miss Cramp and together they chuckled with merriment.

'Well,' sighed Miss Cramp, 'Mr Potter told me that this would be an excellent chance to observe different types of Negroes.'

'It seems to be an excellent chance to observe different types of Caucasians, also,' said Merrit.

'Disgusting, isn't it?' I can't understand why people of apparently our own kind, Mr Merrit . . . It's humiliating, isn't it?'

'They out-Herod the Romans, don't they?'

'Unpardonable. How can we hope to help these others if we set so poor an example ourselves?'

'An excellent point. If we are not careful, instead of helping them, we will find them helping us.'

'Helping us?'

'Yes, Or more. Transforming us. If things go on like this, one of these days this country's going to wake up with dark brown skin and kinky hair.'

'Horrible!'

'Horrible? Why?'

'Oh, Mr Merrit!'

'I really see nothing horrible about it. I rather think the country would enjoy it.'

'Well—I for one shouldn't.'

'But think, Miss Cramp,' he prodded, 'how much better off our country would be—'

'With dark brown skin? I can't imagine—'

'No. Figuratively of course. With a spiritual attitude—an emotional make-up like the Negro's.'

'Just what do you mean?'

'This tropic nonchalance, as Locke calls it. This acceptance of circumstance not with a shrug, like the Oriental, but with a characteristic grin. Nobody laughs at the miseries of life like the Negro. He laughs at himself, at his own pains and dangers and disappointments and oppressions. He accepts things, not with resignation but with amusement. That, it seems to me, should be a most alarming thing for his enemy to see.'

'I don't understand at all.'

'No? Suppose you were fighting somebody, and at every blow you delivered, your antagonist simply grinned and came on. Wouldn't you soon get scared? Wouldn't you begin to lose your nerve? Would you begin wondering if maybe the other fellow wasn't grinning at the futility of your blows—if maybe he wasn't just biding his time in the certainty of his power? How could you wound a fellow who simply laughed? How could you be sure what he was laughing at? Himself? Maybe. But I know I'd begin to think he might be laughing at *me*.'

'It isn't easy to follow you, Mr Merrit. But it seems to me that the Negro would be far better off if he didn't laugh so much, no matter at whom. He doesn't take anything seriously. If he did, if he worried more, I think he'd be far better off today.'

'Well—maybe today, Miss Cramp. But what about tomorrow?'

'What *can* you mean?'

'Wouldn't it be funny, Miss Cramp, if the Negro let his fair-skinned brother—or cousin, to be a trifle more exact—do all the so-called serious work? Build bridges, dig canals, capture natural forces, fly airplanes, amass wealth, evolve society—these are serious things. Wouldn't it be amusing if the Negro let others worry their brains out devising and developing the civilized luxuries of life—while he spent his time simply living, developing nothing but his capacity for enjoyment; and then when the job was finished, stepped in and took complete possession? Suppose—just suppose, for one can never know—that this irrepressible laughter, this resiliency, is caused by the confidence that he will reap what his oppressors have sown?'

'But that's impossible. Where will he ever get the power to take complete possession?'

'Power? Sheer force of numbers—the overwhelming majority of dark skins on the earth. Together with the—er—the effect of climate. If the climate keeps changing, or if people keep exposing themselves to changes in climate, the time will eventually come when there won't be but a few pure skins left . . . Now won't it be positively uproarious if the serious achievements reach their height about then?'

'Well,' she said after a moment, 'I don't think either you or I need worry over that, Mr Merrit. It's altogether too remote. If I can't see that far, I doubt that any Negro can. It need not worry you at all.'

'Quite right. Nobody needs worry over any of it—past, present or future. Its course is unchangeable by anything so futile as people's worry. That's the joker in this very occasion, Miss Cramp. Uplift the Negro? Why, his position is the most profoundly strategic on earth.'

'You really think so?'

'He that is last shall be first.'

'Well, that would certainly be awful, wouldn't it?'

There was silence between them.

Presently Miss Cramp remembered that Merrit had been presented to her as an inured bachelor. She said:

'Mr Merrit, these are serious questions. We must thrash them out some time.'

'I should like nothing better,' he said.

'Do you spend the summer in town?'

'I'm leaving for the country tomorrow but I'll be back by the end of the summer.'

'Then you must come and see me on your return. We shall have so much to discuss.'

'Nothing would give me greater pleasure,' he said, and she saw from the present pleasure in his eyes that he must mean what he was saying.

It gave her a thrill. 'Summers,' she sighed, 'are so long, aren't they?'

'My maid,' said Miss Cramp, 'is a Negress. The first one I have ever had, and I must say, the best. She is very pretty, too. She is so different from what one thinks of on hearing the term, Negress. Extremely pretty, really.'

'And she remains a maid?'

'Why not? It's honest work and very good pay.'

'The pretty ones usually prefer to go on the stage.'

'Oh, Linda wouldn't think of any such thing. You see she was raised in an Episcopal Orphanage and seems to be rather religious. I was quite glad to learn how many Negroes are Episcopalian. I didn't know there were any, did you?'

'Are there?'

'A large number from what this girl says. And what do you think, Mr Merrit? Religious as she is, she never sings spirituals!'

'No? I can't believe it. But she must have some vices?'

'Her only recreation is dancing. Her rector seems to be a very up-to-date person. There are weekly affairs at her church community centre and she always goes.'

'Must be an awfully dull person.'

'On the contrary, extremely interesting. It was through her that I learned of the General Improvement Association. No doubt she is here tonight. In fact, I thought I saw her once just now, down there on the floor, dancing.'

She looked sharply for a prolonged moment, then suddenly exclaimed: 'I did too! There she is, there. That tall one in the gypsy costume—isn't she unusual?'

'The one just starting to dance with the big chap in grey?'

'Yes.'

Merrit too looked sharply. Appreciation of unfamiliar features at that distance in a crowd was difficult, but—

'I've seen that girl somewhere. You say she's your maid?'

'I'm positive that's Linda.'

A moment's rumination then he remembered. Slowly over his face came an expression of elation far more than commensurate with the recognition.

'Miss Cramp,' he said, 'do you by any chance live on Court Avenue?'

'Yes, I do.' She was extremely well pleased. 'I was about to give you my address. However did you know?'

'Why, Miss Cramp,' there was no mistaking his joy, 'we're neighbours!'

'Really? Why, Mr Merrit!'

'You live at three hundred nine, don't you?'

'Yes!'

'And I live at three thirteen—that is I will when I come back to town.'

'How lovely! But—how—?'

'I saw that girl go into your house one morning when I was having some things moved in. She had her own key.'

'Well, isn't this nice, Mr Merrit?' She laughed. 'I suppose

when you saw Linda come in like that, with her own key, you thought you might even have got into a Negro neighbourhood?'

'I admit, I wondered.'

'That would have been tragic.' She lowered her voice. 'I can imagine nothing more awful. To help them is quite all right. To live beside them is quite another matter.'

'It is indeed, Miss Cramp. It is indeed.'

'You need never have any fear of that in Court Avenue. Frankly, we are rather exclusive, you know.'

'I had that in mind when I purchased.'

'And to think we are next door neighbours, Mr Merrit.'

They beamed at each other, each in the delight of his own withheld motive, his own private anticipations; a tableau that was soon interrupted by the noisy return of the two couples that had been dancing. Whereupon, rather suddenly it seemed, Merrit decided that he must leave. He rose to go.

'I shall look forward to your call,' she reminded.

'If I could only be sure you were doing that,' said he, 'you've no idea the pleasure 'twould give me.'

'You can be sure,' she said.

As he left, he chuckled and chided himself:

'Damn shame to worry that poor woman like that—she'll die before the night's over. Somebody'll tell her for sure.'

CHAPTER XII

He had hardly gone when Tony called attention to an odd commotion on the floor below.

'What's going on there?'

Dunn forgot his gallantries to Nora Byle in his eagerness to reach the front of the box. Everyone else pressed forward also to see, Miss Cramp bewilderedly, Gloria Dunn eagerly, Nora Byle amusedly, J. Pennington Potter apprehensively.

'The big guy in grey,' explained Tony. 'Girl—yes, the gypsy costume—suddenly pulled away and he wouldn't let her go. Don't blame him, she's a peach. Look—she jerked away so hard she upset everybody around. They're all stopping to look.'

'See—he's apologizing,' observed Dunn. 'Elaborately. Drunk, I suppose. Drawing quite a crowd, aren't they?'

'Look!' Gloria cried. 'Over on the side—that one. He's starting for them! God—he's big!'

'This looks like a fight,' Dunn said. 'See him move over that floor—why, he actually leaves a wake!'

'There'll be a wake somewhere else if those two big boys meet.'

'That's Linda!' exclaimed Miss Cramp.

'Who?'

'Linda—my maid—!'

'Who? The gypsy?'

'Yes. Oh, however did she—?'

'Poor kid can't get out of the crowd. Grey suit's right on her heels, protesting. Some sheik.'

A suppressed cry of 'Fight!' went about. There were gasps and quick searching looks of alarm. The orchestra distant, oblivious, struck up, 'Take Yo' Fingers Off It.'

Then those who from above focused attention on the little

crowd of dancers around Patmore and Linda, saw Shine succeed in breaking through to meet Linda as she endeavoured to escape; saw Patmore look up, draw back, shrink, stand for a moment uncertain, as if both eager and loath to flee; saw Shine and Linda halt, facing each other, the girl distressed and surprised, the man grim and tense; saw her then fling herself impulsively toward him, uttering an inaudible but obvious plea; saw him catch her, thrust her behind him, and turn back—to find Patmore gone; saw Patmore, already out of the crowd, moving with surreptitious speed toward one of the lateral exits.

Then they saw the collection of observers disperse, Shine and Linda moving off together. Couples casually resumed dancing and the stream, as if undisturbed, resumed its course.

Everyone in J. Pennington Potter's box sighed prodigiously.

'Marvellous!' commented Mr Dunn.

'Marvellous!' echoed Mrs Dunn.

And after a moment, 'Marvellous!' cried J. Pennington Potter, like one who at last sees the light.

Miss Cramp found that Nora Byle had dropped into the chair beside her, and that insistent questions in her own head clamoured for utterance at this opportunity. She was however quite un-prepared to make the most of this opportunity, because she had never considered that certain methods of approach might be useless. She thought she had only to ask, and it would be given.

Between members of opposed races, however, the subject of race is difficult, almost indeed delicate. Neither party quite wholly sacrifices his illusions about his own people nor admits his ignorance about the other. The conversation, therefore, becomes a series of unwitting affronts, mutual mistrusts and suppressed indignations increasingly harder to bear, all at last it futilely breaks off with both parties ready to burst—each inwardly smouldering at the other's unforgivable ignorance and tactlessness. Here is the hedonistic paradox if anywhere, that one best learns the facts of a race by ignoring the fact of race.

If Nordic and Negro wish truly to know each other, let them discuss not Negroes and Nordics; let them discuss Greek lyric poets of the fourth century B.C.

Wise observers sense this and avoid the crassly obvious. But Miss Cramp was too deeply sincere and too genuinely curious to exercise tact. She ventured the usual opening:

'Your people seem to enjoy themselves so.'

'They do seem to,' agreed Nora with slightly different emphasis.

'You mean they really don't?'

'Well, some folks laugh to keep from crying, you know.'

Miss Cramp thought she saw in this a personal confession. This exquisite creature of blended blood must indeed be very unhappy. The personal implication surely invited intimacy. She said sympathetically:

'I suppose you speak from experience, my dear. How much white blood have you?'

Nora suppressed a gasp, then said too, too gently: 'I don't quite know, Miss Cramp.' And added sweetly as if returning a greeting: 'How much black have you?'

Miss Cramp did not suppress her gasp, she merely prolonged it into a sputtering little laugh and exclaimed: 'What a sense of humour you have, Mrs Byle!'

'Yes, haven't I?'

'I was just saying to Mr Merrit,' Miss Cramp persevered, 'that so much can be done for your people. Not for you, of course. Or Mr Potter. But the great majority. You have heard that remark of somebody's, no doubt, that most Negroes are just three jumps ahead of the monkeys?'

'White monkeys?' smiled Nora.

'Oh, Mrs Byle—how amusing! But seriously. I think there is much to be done, don't you?'

'Oh, yes indeed—'

'I was telling Mr Merrit about my maid, Linda. The girl we were watching down there just now—I must scold her severely for that. But—why, do you know, I had no idea what really marvellous servants they make. After having Linda I wouldn't think of having any other kind of maid. I've had Irish and French and German, but none of them were nearly so good as Linda.'

'The best maid I ever had,' disagreed Mrs Byle, 'was a German girl.'

That Mrs Byle should have had a maid at all seemed to come as a shock to Miss Cramp, a shock unrelieved by the casual reference to the maid's Nordicity. 'You had a—a German maid?'

'Yes. A wonderful worker. But I had to let her go finally. I simply couldn't endure her English.'

'Well—' said Miss Cramp '—well—anyway I prefer coloured girls to any of the others.'

'Perhaps because they're American.'

'American? Oh—well, yes, they are—in a way.'

Nora bit her lip.

'I'm so int'rested in the Negro problem, genuinely int'rested, you know,' Miss Cramp continued.

'How do you plan to solve it?'

'Well there is the labour aspect of it. As I said before they make excellent servants. Why not have more Negro servants?'

'Porters and scullions and chamber maids?'

'Exactly. It may be possible to increase the numbers of such workers.'

'I don't see how increasing the numbers helps solve any problem.'

'Well—'

'Why not try to change them over into governesses and secretaries?'

'Oh, my dear—who would want a coloured secretary?'

There was an awkward silence between them which neither the beating of tom-toms nor the rain falling on banana leaves seemed to relieve. Eventually Miss Cramp said:

'You met Mr Merrit, of course?'

'Met him?'

'Didn't you, my dear? A fine type of American gentleman—'

'Why, I've known Fred Merrit for years.'

The familiarity in this remark struck Miss Cramp as unseemly.

'Yes,' remarked she. 'He said he'd worked among Negroes all his life.'

Nora experienced first resentment at the implication of this supremely thoughtless comment, then, conflicting with it, amusement at the realization that Fred had evidently been masquerading at this lady's expense.

'Is there any reason,' she said, 'why he shouldn't work all his life among his own people?'

The statement transfixed Miss Cramp like a lance, and the swift change of mien from complacency to unbelieving horror was so violent that Nora almost felt remorse at having occasioned it.

'What!' Miss Cramp managed a faint little squeal.

'You weren't under the impression that Mr Merrit was *not* a Negro, were you?'

'Why—I—I didn't know. I thought—'

'I'm sure he wouldn't have deceived you intentionally.'

'But Mrs Byle—his complexion—his skin is so fair—'

'Yes. He even has green eyes.'

'I should never have thought—'

'You ought to have noticed his hair, "my dear".'

'His hair?'

'It's all that betrays him and you have to look close to see that it really is kinky.'

At this point the irate Buckram Byle made his presence felt. No one had been paying much attention to Mr Byle. And so, as much to attract notice as to punish his wife, he now called loudly to her that he had long since indicated his intention to go home and had no idea of letting her ignore it. Nora, having topped off an excellent evening, raised no objection.

'I must go,' she said to Miss Cramp. 'It's really so very nice knowing you—er—my dear—'

Miss Cramp sat staring about with eyes that comprehended nothing, the turbulence in her own mind confusing every perception: eddies and currents of heads swirling about in the stream below her; constantly shifting, insane patterns of colour, coming and going; wanton cries, prodigal jests, abandoned Negro laughter; and the orchestra, remotely dominant, sustaining it all with a ceaseless rhythm like the pulse of a pounding heart.

All this the mad accompaniment of a pitiless cycle of reflections:

'A Negro on Court Avenue and I asked him to call—they'll blame *me*. A Negro on Court Avenue—'

JIVE

CHAPTER XIII

DESPITE the genial atmosphere of Pat's pool room, the substantial goodwill of the table over which the vari-coloured ivory balls rolled, the cosy cheer of the green-shaded low-hung light, Jinx and Bubber could not discuss even the weather in agreement.

'Sure is hot,' Bubber had commented, missing a shot and wiping a glistening brow on his arm.

'Don't blame the weather jes' 'cause you can't shoot pool,' returned Jinx. 'I likes warm weather like this.'

'Can't see what fo'.'

'Well—we got to work outdoors, ain't we?'

'Yea—in d' heat.'

'Aw right. In warm weather you can find some place outdoors to cool off, but when it's cold, damn if you can find any place outdoors to get warm.'

'Cold weather fo' mine,' disagreed Bubber. '

'Shuh!'

'Yessir. We got to wear clothes, ain't we?'

'Uh-huh.'

'Well, when it's cold you can put on enough to get warm, but when it's hot, damn if you can take off enough to get cool!'

Jinx pretended to ignore this unanswerable point by bending far and low over a long corner shot.

'Number eight,' he called, signifying his intention to pocket the black ball. 'Sure loves to make this eight-ball—jes' like punchin' you in the nose.' And he made it, cueing the ball with exaggerated vehemence.

Henry Patmore sauntered up. 'Where's yo' boy?' he inquired.

'What you mean—Shine?'

'Don't mean his brother.'

'Hell,' said Bubber. 'Ain't seen that boogy a single night since the dance.'

'Jivin' a dickty gal now,' explained Jinx, regarding the table critically, with a sidewise twist of his head. 'Bringin' me mud.'

'Yea?' said Pat.

'Dickty?' scoffed Bubber. 'What's dickty 'bout her?'

'Ev'rything,' said Jinx preparing to try a difficult combination, '—compared to him.'

'Mean the gal he picked up at the Casino th' other night?' asked Pat.

'Don't mean her sister,' assented Bubber. 'She ain't nobody's dickty, though. Powerful easy to look at but jes' ordinary K.M. right on.'

'She may be a K.M.,' conceded Jinx, 'but if there's anythin' ordinary 'bout her, I ain't seen it.'

'Got the big boy goin', huh?' grinned Pat.

'Goin' and comin',' said Bubber; then to Jinx, 'How long you go'n' look at that ball, man? Go on—shoot!'

'Who d' hell's makin' this shot?'

'Ain't nobody makin' it, far as I can see.'

Pat smiled metallically and moved off. Jinx called and shot, dispersing a cluster of balls, of which not one found its way into a pocket. Whereupon Bubber echoed their cackling laughter, revealing his stretch of bare upper gum between the two lateral stumps.

'One of these times when you laff like that,' prophesied Jinx with great ill-humour, 'I'm go'n' bust you in the mouth so hard you'll grow yo'self some teeth.'

Bubber's scorn was superlative. 'You might stick out a fist,' he warned, 'but you won't draw nothin' back but a nub.' He busily chalked his cue, surveying the pattern of balls with enormous gravity.

'Yo' legs is so bowed,' Jinx observed, 'that you wear yo' shoes out on the sides. Better stop laffin' at me like that. One of these times I bet I'm go'n' to run you knock-kneed.'

'I wouldn't run that fast,' returned Bubber, squatting to squint over the table, 'after nobody.'

'Ain't talking 'bout after—talkin' 'bout from.'

'From?' Bubber stood erect. 'Me run from you?'

'You do have bright moments, dark as you is.'

'Brother, let me tell you sump'm. If it ever even looks like I'm runnin' from you, there won't be but one explanation fo' it.' Bubber paused oratorically. 'Because you done outrun me so fast you mus' caught up with me again.' Wherewith he made his shot.

Jinx solemnly shook his head. 'It sure would be awful hard,' he said.

'What?'

'Awful hard on old man Isaacs.'

'What you talkin' 'bout?'

'To lose two good men at once.'

'Boy, you done gone crazy?'

'No. I was jes' thinking—'

'Oh. That's different.'

'—I'm go'n' to have to kill you sooner or later—only way to get along with you. And that gal is jes' 'bout ruined Shine—he ain't never go'n' to be no mo' good.'

'Shuh!' scoffed the other. 'She might scratch 'im a little, but ain't no gal go'n' put no deep dents in that jasper. He ain't got no place soft enough.'

'The hell he ain't. Know where I seen 'im goin' tonight, dressed up like a monkey-back?'

'Where?'

'Seen 'im go'n' in that 'Piscopal church.'

Bubber stared a moment, then proceeded disgustedly with his sighting. 'What d' hell you 'spect a man to believe?' he commented.

'Swear I did. Not the main door. You know that side door—'nother buildin' it is, where they have dances and basket-ball and ev'rything else they scared to do in the church itself. Call it the 'immunity-house' or sump'm like that.'

'Yea?' Bubber dropped his stick. So long as Shine hadn't entered the main door of the church, the matter was credible enough to be startling.

'I sure did.'

Bubber slowly shook his head. 'Bye-bye, blackbird.' Then, still somewhat suspicious, 'Where was you when you saw 'im?'

'Followin' 'im. Thought he might need some help if he was out sheikin'.'

'Well, kiss my Aunt Anne's preserves!' Bubber pondered the imponderable a moment, slowly recovering his stick and most of his incredulity. 'Aw, don't be no fool. That jigaboo's jes' jivin'.'

'Maybe. But, same time, ain't nothin' to hinder *her* from jivin', too. And when two folks gets to jivin' each other, first thing you know sump'm happens.'

'Sump'm go'n' happen all right, but 'tain't go'n' happen to *him*.' Bubber resumed his survey of the balls scattered widely by Jinx's miss. 'Bet I'm go'n' run off all the rest,' he wagered.

Jinx, however, had become philosophical. 'Jes' goes to show you, see? There's a guy what's so big and hard he can't be had. Most o' these gals 'round here tries their damnedest to make him—but he jes' don't fall. No mo' than he fell that time Spider Webb cut at him and missed and nearly got broke in two. So hard. So hard his spit bounces. Says to me—say, "Jinx you speckled-hide ostrich you, women ain't no different from men—only worse. You gotta be tough and tight, boy. Once they see you slippin', it's yo' hiney from then on—they'll put the locks on you and throw the key away. But if you be hard with 'em, they ain't no trouble at all." Yea. And then this one come along. She's diff'rent, see? Act all dickty and ev'rything. High-hats 'im. K.M. all right—but not jes' ordinary K.M.—*Dickty* K.M., see? That jes' 'bout gets 'im. He gives up without a struggle.'

'How do you know he's given up?' Bubber's doubt persisted.

'Went in the damn church after 'er, didn't he?'

'That ain't nothin'. I've seen women I'd go in worse places than that after.'

'Yea?'

'No lie. And they wasn't near as easy to gaze on as that sister, either. Dicky—shuh—that ain't got nothin' to do with it. It's that ball-bearin' movement, that's what.'

'Damn if it makes *him* run any smoother. One day he's good natured as a puppy-dawg, 'nother he's evil as a black cat. Never seen a man change so. She done put it on 'im all right!'

'Bet he go'n' to put sump'm on her, too.'

'Damn if I believe it. She'll have 'im go'n' in the *main* door next. This is serious.'

'So's this,' said Bubber, who had meanwhile run off seven balls, unnoticed. Thereupon, mimicking perfectly, he duplicated the shot which Jinx had made earlier with such exaggerated vehemence. The ball was the last on the table, and it sped to an already full pocket eagerly, greeting its fellows with a cheerful 'clack!'

Bubber looked at his victim with a grin. Jinx frowned unbelievingly at the clean green table top and, as Bubber broke into his customary guffaw, stood scowling malevolently at him, as if undecided whether to dispose of him at once or let him live a little time longer.

CHAPTER XIV

'BABY—' began Shine.

'Don't call me baby!' exploded Linda.

''Smatter? Don't you like children?'

'It sounds so—common.'

'I couldn't mean it that way—you know that.'

'How do I know what you could mean?'

'Couldn't ever say nothin' common 'bout you. Couldn't even think it. "Baby" is a nice name.'

'Think so? Well, save it for your sweetheart.'

'I did,' he grinned.

'Wrong number,' she said, but she smiled.

'That was my lucky day,' he mused. 'What did Pat say to you that night? Why wouldn't you ever tell me?'

Thus, while Bubber and Jinx discussed them over a pool table, Shine and Linda strolled slowly along the west walk of Riverside Drive. A few blocks east lay Harlem, black and sullen, too uncomfortable by far for dancing this hot August night, even the distant and circumspect dancing permitted in a parish hall. Nearer was Court Avenue, whither the present roundabout walk led.

Here on the Drive it was cool. Occasional meandering couples passed arm in arm, and on the long benches that rimmed the walk, facing the Hudson, still others made love, oblivious and unashamed.

'Huh?' insisted Shine.

'Nothing to tell,' murmured Linda.

'Must be. Saw enough myself to know that.'

'What did you see?'

'Well, I'm lookin' for Pat myself, see? He's jes' pulled a crooked deal on me a minute before, and I'm askin' for 'im. Well, you know the crowd—only people you can find is them

you ain't lookin' for. I'm standin' at the foot of the stairs lookin'
for that grey suit. Finally I sees it way across the floor—and
damn if the sleeves ain't 'round *your* waist.'

'Stop swearing—'

'That sort o' cramps my style, see? Don't want to mix you
up in anything. But I got to have some o' Patmore. So I'm
standin' there wonderin' what the top card is and lookin' at
you. Then I see you don't look so good—kinda like a kitten
some rough kid won't turn loose. Turnin' yo' head this way and
d' other way and sorta pullin' away from this bird even though
you keep on dancin'. And I smoke *him* over, and he's grinnin'
like a Chess-cat with a mouse—a nice young tender mouse, see
what I mean? Well, I've seen that grin before, and I know it
like I know my landlady's. Only, any time I see a guy grin like
that before, I jes' feel kinda sorry for 'im for bein' such a sap.
This time I ain't sorry. That same grin turns me cold.'

He paused so long that she urged him on. 'You didn't stay
cold long.'

'No—and why? Because the next thing I know you stop
dancin' right in the middle of a step and look at him like you
didn't know anybody's breath could smell so bad—'

'Oh!'

'But it don't worry Mr Patmore none. He jes' pushes his face
on out at you, and makes another crack. That's the one I want
to know about, because that's the time you jerks away from him
like as if he burnt your fingers. Meantime the kacks is closin'
in and you can't make a quick getaway. And when I come to,
I'm down on the floor haulin' it through the crowd.'

'There's an empty bench under that tree,' discovered Linda.
They sat down, deep in the shadow of foliage, and during a
moment's silence looked out over the river. Directly opposite
loomed the Palisades, like a wide and gloomy black fortress,
clear-limned against a sky dimly pale with an adolescent moon.
Below, the dark water glittered a smile that derided the callow
moon's wooing.

'Well, I don't know jes' what happens then,' Shine presently continued, 'but when I reach for Pat, he's breezed. Never see a man catch so much air so fast. Then you looked like you was go'n' cry and said you wanted to go home or some place—so I took you.'

'I didn't know what I was saying.'

'I did.'

'Seen 'im since?' she asked.

'No. That's why I want the dope. When I crown 'im I want to tell 'im exactly what he's king of.'

'You mustn't bother him—let him alone.'

'I got a picture o' myself lettin' any guy alone that gets fly with my girl.'

'Your *what*?'

'You ain't blind.'

'Well of all the nerve!'

'Hit me,' he invited contritely, exposing a rugged cheek.

'Your—' She was overcome. 'Well what do you know about that?'

He answered her literally. 'Nothin', but I'm willin' to learn.'

She averted her face to hide her smile. 'I couldn't have been your—anything—anyway, then. Didn't even know your name.'

'Well,' he said with elaborate innuendo, 'maybe I *was* jes' a little bit previous.'

'What do you mean!'

'Nothin' lady—nothin'. Don't get so excited. I jes' mean to say, you know my name now, that's all.'

'Well, you needn't think—'

'And now *that* storm is over, how 'bout the dope?'

'What dope?'

'What did Pat say?'

She was silent a long time. The lights of a homeward bound excursion boat broke through the river's moonlit smile, but when the ship had passed, the smile was still ironically there. Wraiths of music and laughter drifted shoreward.

'If you promise not to get in trouble over it—'

'Promise anything. Spill it.'

'You know he had said there were prizes for the best costumes.'

'Yea—and he was a judge.'

'Yes. Well, I believed it. When he came back for the second dance, he was lit. I'd asked some other folks about it.'

'The Sunday School boys you was dancin' with?'

'No! The girls I came with. I asked them about the prizes and nobody knew anything about 'em. But I wasn't sure and I didn't want to offend him if he was telling the truth. So instead of asking him right out, I said, "I thought you told me there were going to be prizes," just as if I'd already found out there wasn't. And all he did was to grin with all those brass teeth of his. That made me mad, and I told him what I thought of anybody that would do anything like that—and—'

'Yea?'

'Well, finally when I saw he really had been lying, I stopped dancing and tried to walk off but he held me and people began to look. Then he said—'

'Said what?'

'He said I needn't act so disappointed over losin' twenty-five dollars—that he was a judge, all right—and—'

Her voice became low and hard. Unconsciously they drew closer together.

'And what?' he said after a moment.

'Well—he offered me twenty-five dollars.'

Silence enfolded them, deeper than the shadow. It seemed an endless period before someone laughed in the darkness a distance away. Thereupon the leaves of the tree overhead heaved a gentle, prolonged sigh.

They sat for a long time wordless, looking across the sardonic Hudson.

CHAPTER XV

IT HAPPENED the next morning that Linda ran out of sugar, discovering her predicament only a few minutes before Miss Cramp's breakfast was to be served. There were, of course, no grocery stores within three blocks of exclusive Court Avenue, and while ordinarily Miss Cramp would have waited without complaint till the errand was run, today the situation was awkward: Miss Cramp had company, a lady from Baltimore, Maryland; a friend, to be sure, but a friend whose breakfast, must not be delayed by the delinquencies of a coloured maid.

Linda, therefore, following professional tradition, resolved to borrow sufficient from her next-door neighbour to tide over the temporary lack, and was already on the kitchen-porch going to the Irish girl next door when she saw a Negro woman beating rugs in the back yard of the second house. She had her own curiosity about that particular house, because she had overheard Miss Cramp and the present guest discussing it, and she decided that this was her chance at an opening that would satisfy that curiosity. She would borrow the sugar from the coloured woman.

It was thus that she made the acquaintance of Fred Merrit's housekeeper, Mrs Arabella Fuller.

'Drop in any time,' invited Mrs Fuller, who was a genial, lonesome soul, not too insistent on the social distinctions between housekeepers and maids, and who would apparently have had more to say had Linda been less obviously pressed for time.

'Thanks,' smiled Linda. 'This afternoon. My folks are going to a show.'

And so that afternoon found her and Mrs Fuller conversing in the Merrit kitchen with all the ease and confidence of a much more extended friendship.

Without conscious effort Mrs Arabella Fuller would have arrested any cartoonist's attention. Her profile was a series of adjoining semicircles—a large one for the bulbous forehead, then a succession of smaller, approximately equal ones, forming from above downward nose, upper lip, lower lip, first chin and second chin. From above downward, moreover, this series slanted unanimously rearward, so that the forehead bulged and the chins receded, and the general attitude was that of one caught in the act of swallowing half a banana.

This profile only stated the motif on which Mrs Fuller as a whole was composed. Every outline of every part was a perfect semicircle, and so on integration she naturally became a cluster of hemispheres. There were, to be sure, unanticipatedly sudden constrictions about her at points: between chins, for example, at wrists, at waist and at ankles. But these repressions were futile, for on either side of each constriction the flesh triumphantly bulged. They simply heightened the lady's agglomerate bulbosity.

Out of the midst of this there escaped on occasion, an asthmatic wheeze. This confab was such an occasion, and it revealed at once that the asthma in no way discouraged Mrs Fuller's flow of language.

'Yes, indeed, child. Any time you want anything like that jes' come right on over and get it—we always has plenty ev'rything on hand. That's one thing about Mr Merrit—he sure believes in eating. Reckon that's why he so thin. And it makes him mad as a wet hen to run outta anything and that's why I always has plenty ev'rything on hand. So anytime you run out, jes' come on over and I'll trust you to keep account o' ev'rything you get.' She fanned her shining round brown face with a limp dishcloth and smiled as she paused for breath. The smile revealed a shining row of white teeth, each of them just half a circle.

'It's nice here,' Linda observed, looking about.

''Deed it is. And Mr Merrit's such a nice man to work for. 'Cause he have his big times and so on, and he like his toddy now an' then a little too good, and every once in a while he gets tied up with some woman or 'nother, but 'course that's natural, him bein' a bachelor and havin' so much money. I just shuts my eyes and says nothing, 'cause 'tain't none my business, and he ain't never said nothin' out the way to *me*, y' understand, so I jes' do my work and go on. You know how 'tis—you must see and don't see.' There was another reluctant pause.

'Indeed so,' agreed Linda, already somewhat apprehensive at the conflict in Mrs Fuller's speech. It appeared that while Mrs Fuller's laboured respiration sought to shorten her sentences, her sentences had a will of their own and simply refused to be shortened. Linda already found herself drawing deep sympathetic but wholly useless breaths.

''Course there's a lot o' folks what don't like to work fo' coloured, I understand that, and I don't know as I would myself if it had to be some these uppity coloured women what ain't never been used to nothin' and jes' now got sump'm and think they so much more 'n ev'rybody else. Take fo' 'n instant that Sarah Bell Long, what's always riding 'round in Cornelia Bond's auto. I knowed her when she was a baby—knowed her father and mother before her. Neither one of 'em wasn't nothin'. Old man Bell run a saloon in Augusta till he made enough to buy up half the black belt; then he retired, got religious, gave the church a lot o' the money and got hisself preached into the kingdom and his wife along with 'im. Then this Sarah gal married this young doctor—least, he was then—and set him up in business, and when they got tired livin' down there 'cause some them women liked his treatment too well, why, they up and comes to New York. And havin' plenty money naturally they starts right out at the top. But I always say the top ain't but a little way from the bottom—can't be—'tain't been risin' long enough. And ain't none of us so much better'n the rest of us that we can afford to get uppity 'bout it. And that's why I jes' couldn't stand workin' around nobody that act that way. Ain't no sense in it. But Mr Fred ain't like that. Ain't nobody in Harlem got no better things than Mr Fred is, and some them things up in the country he brought back with 'im all the way from Europe and France and them places 'way yonder 'cross the water. You'll see 'em when they get here—he always have 'em sent in town fo' the winter. And ain't nobody in New York got nothing no better, but it don't turn his head none. Look like he jes' buy things to spend his money and when he get 'em that ends it. All except one thing—a picture of his mother. Least, I think it must be his mother, though he ain't never told me so. But he stands and looks at that picture fo' hours at a time, seems like. I believe 'twould near 'bout kill 'im to lose it. But he sure is a nice man to work fo'—don't never bother you 'bout nothin'.'

Linda decided it would be less exhausting to do some of the talking herself. She hastened to inject at this pause, 'I should think it would be nice, working for a man, anyhow. Bet he isn't fussy 'n' everything like an old woman—'specially an old maid. Gee!'

'Yo' madam ain't never had a husband of her own?'

'Uh-uh.'

'How come she ain't?'

'Guess she never knew whether a man wanted her or her money.'

'What diff'rence that make?'

'Well, I guess she figured if he *did* want it, she didn't want *him*, and if he *didn't* want it, there must be something wrong with him. That just made the whole thing sorta hopeless.'

'She nice to work fo'?'

Linda saw that the way to prevent Mrs Fuller from talking herself to death was to keep her asking questions. 'Well,' she answered, 'she could be worse. Nicest part is she lives all alone and that makes the work light. But she get sick over the least little thing and she spends a lot o' time in bed. She just got over a three weeks' spell yesterday—only reason she got up was because this friend from Baltimore was coming last night You can't imagine what made her sick this time.'

'Is this visitor a gentleman friend?'

'Nope.'

'Then what?' Linda could sense that Mrs Fuller was merely nosing for an opening through which she could break for a long unobstructed run of speech.

'She found out that your boss was a jig, and it put her in bed for three weeks. I didn't know what the trouble was till last night and I heard her talking to this Baltimore woman. The way she's carrying on you'd think the house had turned to a hospital for smallpox. Indeed it wouldn't surprise me to see it burnt down any time.'

'What you mean, child?'

'Well, you know how much fays like to have jigs move in next door to 'em.'

'Indeed I do. I remember years ago—'

''Specially if it's a nice neighbourhood. They'd do most anything to get 'em out. Look at what they did to that man in Staten Island last fall. Ku-Kluxed him. It was even in the fay papers, how they burnt the man's house down while he was out. I believe Miss Cramp is wild enough to do the self-same thing—or have it done.'

'Have it done—how you mean?'

'*Pay* somebody to do it.'

'No!'

'Bet she'd offer to pay *you* to do it.'

'And I bet I'd smack her from here to yonder, too!'

'Well, there's plenty of fay toughs around here—not right on this street but near enough—and I bet she could get somebody to get *them*. Then she wouldn't be suspected. Everybody'd think it was like that house on One Hundred Forty-ninth Street somebody put dynamite under.'

'What?'

'Didn't you read about it?'

'No!'

'It was in *The Black Issue*—oh, a long time ago now. Man

bought a house on One Hundred Forty-ninth Street and they dared him to move in. Sent letters and all. But he went on in. And less 'n a week after he moved in, they blew him out—bajooey!—just like that.'

'Well I never in all my life!'

'Indeed they did. And Miss Cramp is worried and mad and everything. You ought to have heard her last night talking to this southern woman.'

Linda decidedly had the floor now and she did not intend to relinquish it.

'She's from some little dump in Maryland, but she swears she lives in Baltimore—as if even that was anything to brag about. She's just like Miss Cramp, only more so. Well, you know one time Miss Cramp asked me a lot o' dumb questions about shines and I gave her a lot of dumb answers and she went and joined the G.I.A. to find out for herself. And for doing it!'

'Say what?'

'Last night she was telling this other one all about it, and I mean they just carried on. Miss Cramp says, "My dear, I'm in the most awful trouble—you simply must tell me what to do."

'This other one is the funniest thing—talks like a jig fresh from down home. First time I ever heard a fay talk like a shine—I was never so surprised. She says, "'Deed, honey, with all yo' money I cain't imagine what could worry you."

'Then Miss Cramp says, "If something isn't done pretty quick this whole neighbourhood's going black."

'"What!" says this Mrs Parmalee—that's the other one.

'"And that isn't the worst of it," Miss Cramp sniffles. "The worst of it is that *I'll* get the *blame* for it."

'"You'll get the blame fo' it?"

'"I'm not responsible, really. But I got interested in the welfare of Negroes and joined a mixed organization for the improvement of conditions among them, you know. Well, naturally, I had to go about among them—"

"'I've always told you charity'd get you in trouble.'"

"'Well it certainly has. I went, on a friend's advice too, to see how they acted in their own surroundings and there were both white and coloured people in the box with me.'"

"'What?'"

"'And one of them was the man that has bought a house almost next *door* to me here on Court Avenue—and Irene, he intends to *live* in it!'"

'And Irene says, just like a jig for the world—"Well, bless mah soul!"

"'But my dear,' says Miss Cramp, "that isn't the worst of it. You can't imagine. My dear, I asked him to call.'"

"'You what?'"

"'I thought he was white. He looked like it. He's blonder than I am.'"

"'How'd you find out he wasn't?' says Irene.

"'Someone else told me after he'd gone.'"

"'Well, Agatha,' says Irene, "if you didn't have no better sense than to invite a strange man to call—'"

"'But he was so nice, Irene—'"

"'Agatha!'"

"'I mean—you wouldn't have suspected, yourself. And, Irene, he swore he was coming, too.'"

"'You don't mean you actually think he will?'"

"'Why won't he?'"

"'A nigger ought to know better.'"

"'Well, this is New York, you know.'"

"'I don't care what this is—'"

"'Anyway, suppose neighbours of mine see my name on the literature of this organization. As soon as this man moves in, I'll be accused.'"

'Then Mrs Parmalee looks real evil and says, "He wouldn't move in down in Baltimore City, I bet you."

"'He will here though,' Miss Cramp says. "And if he does, I declare I'll move out. I couldn't bear the shame.'"

"'Thought you so anxious to uplift 'em?" Irene says, and I nearly split.

"'Well," answers Agatha, "it's one thing to help them and quite another to live beside them as equals. And to have everyone in the street *blaming* me—I simply couldn't bear it.'"

"'Mean to move?'"

"'What else—?'"

"'Move all these here beautiful old things you've accumulated and your daddy before you? Leave this house he left you, where you've lived all your life? Mean to just get up and walk out and do nothing else at all?'"

"'But that's why I'm telling *you*, Irene. What else *can* I do?'"

'I'll tell you what else you can do. You can—' Then she stops a minute and says in a lower voice, "That maid of yours likely to be eavesdropping?'

'So of course then I had to catch air'. Certainly wish I knew what she told her to do.'

The oppression of Mrs Fuller's compulsory silence together with the emotions excited by what she had heard by this time had her in the throes of a fit. She panted and gasped while Linda paused to look on with curiosity and some alarm. The girl's apprehension cost her the floor.

'Know what you ought to do?' Mrs Fuller managed to a get in; to which there was but one thing to say:

'What?'

'You ought to refuse to stay in that woman's house another minute. You ought to up and leave.'

'And go where?'

'Ain't you got—?' Mrs Fuller stopped short, struck with a notion. The notion flowered into an idea. She grinned a half-moon grin, scalloped with tiny lesser half-moons, drew breath prodigiously, and delivered herself:

'Child, I'm go'n' need a maid right here. I done told Mr Merrit already, and he say soon's he come in town it'd be all right. Y'see we been livin' in a 'partment all along and 'twasn't but six rooms and I could take care of everything with a little day help, but now with all this house it's go'n' be too much fo' me and I don't feel none too good nohow, so Mr Merrit say it'll be fine and to get a good girl and make sure she ain't too ugly 'cause he didn't want his stomach turned, and bless my soul if I ain't forgot all about it till this very minute. Now if you ain't got no objection to workin' fo' y'own people, he's a fine man to work fo' and 'll never give you no trouble—least, not 'bout yo' work. 'Cause you kinda pretty fo' a maid, but I reckon you can take good care o' yo'self, and anyhow he's a gentleman. So here's a job ready and waitin' fo' you if you want it.'

'How much?' said Linda. 'I'm getting eighteen—that's pretty good, you know.'

'Shuh, child, he'd give you twenty—jes' to be givin' you more 'n you been gettin'. He pays me twenty-five and says it's a heap cheaper 'n marryin', but I jes' tells 'im he needn't hint at me like that 'cause there's some things he couldn't pay me to do—'

'Twenty dollars!'

'Sure, child. All I got to do is tell 'im—'

Linda jumped up. 'You mean it?'

'Mean every word of it and you'd have lots mo' time to yo'self, too.'

'Honest? Do you think—' An old ambition raised its head. '—Do you think maybe I could go to night school sometimes and learn to run a typewriter?'

This time Mrs Fuller stopped breathing altogether. 'Do which?'

'I don't want to be a K.M. all my life.'

'Aimin' to better yo'self, huh?'

Linda was afraid she had made the wrong move here, but it was too late to change. She nodded with exaggerated vigour.

'Glory be!' was Mrs Fuller's surprising comment. 'Glad to see it, child, glad to see it. Does me good to see one of our young girls what wants to better herself. Our girls ain't got no ambition, no ambition at all, 'ceptin' to go on the stage or dance in a cabaret or some such thing as that.'

There followed a lengthy dissertation on the laziness of 'our' girls, to which Linda listened, eagerly impatient. Finally Mrs Fuller concluded with:

"Deed, child, that's fine and I'm glad to see it and I'll help you all I can—you can get off most every night—and I bet Mr Fred'll give you all the encouragement in the world and maybe one them typewritin' things to boot. Well, want to try it? You can start soon's he get back. How 'bout it?'

'How 'bout it?' Linda exulted. 'How 'bout it? Oh boy!'

CHAPTER XVI

WHILE he couldn't compare it with the Lafayette Theatre of course, still Joshua Jones considered it a pretty good show. At least it would have been if the dumb-bells hadn't jumped up and down so often.

It began with music, a chorus singing far away behind the audience outside the church, it seemed. The singing came nearer and entered at the rear, and Shine obeyed the impulse to turn and look, but before he could determine what the trick in it was, Linda pinched his arm sharply and brought him about, puzzled and resentful, to see her shaking her bowed head with ill-concealed vigour. Thereupon he noticed that everyone else stood like Linda, motionless, with lowered head, as if it wasn't proper to look and he wondered what manner of performance this was, which one might attend, but on which one might not gaze.

Into his surreptitious sidewise vision first came two kids carrying enormous lighted candles. The kids wore black bordered white robes and seemed to have an awfully hard time waiting for the rest of the procession to catch up. Then came the leading man, distinguished by his sedate bearing and singular position, also in a flowing white robe. Shine saw the lean face with its sharp profile and pallid skin and concluded that this guy didn't much enjoy his job.

There passed, following the leading man, a countless succession of increasingly taller couples, all in robes, all singing lustily without ever once consulting the books they carried before them: not much of a chorus, since the costumes made it almost impossible to distinguish the chorines from the chorats. Good singing though, funny, slow, no pep, but something about it.

Eventually they all found their places up front. There followed fifteen minutes of many and mysterious diversions:

The two kids playing a game with the candles—lighting a lot more candles arched over the stage, seeing who could light the most. That ended in a draw. The leading man singing a solo with the whole chorus coming to his rescue every time he paused for breath or seemed to falter. The leading man was all right, but he sure couldn't sing. More singing—this was better—with the audience joining tardily in. Much jumping up and down on the part of everybody. And now the taking up of admission—Shine exhibited a quarter to Linda questioningly. She nodded and presently he dropped the coin into the proffered box, murmuring, 'Well, y' can't go wrong for a quarter.'

This marked the end of the first act. The leading man rose in his place at one side of the stage and began to talk. His deep-set black eyes seemed to fasten themselves on Shine, who soon found himself watching and listening intently. If ever as a youngster he had heard this tale at the Orphanage Sunday School, it had been in so different a guise that now it appeared brand new.

He told it to Jinx and Bubber later, and told it with great accuracy:

'It was all about a bird named Joshua, a great battler some years back. A general, see? Led his own army, and how! This bunch could lick anything that marked time, see?

'Well, this Joshua thought he was the owl's bowels, till one day he run up against a town named Jericho. Town—this place was a flock o' towns. It was the same thing to that part o' the country that New York is to this. It was the works. Without it the rest of the outfit jes' simply couldn't go 'round

'But try and get in. This burg has walls around it so thick that the gals could have their jazz houses on top—not a bad idea at all: if a tight Oscar held out on 'em, they could just let him out on the wrong side o' the wall. And here this red hot papa, Joshua, who's never had his damper turned down yet—here he is up against that much wall—and the damn thing don't budge.

'Now comes the castor oil—the part that's hard to swaller but that does you good if you do. Joshua asks the Lord what the hell to do about this wall. And the Lord says, "Josh, you're my boy, see? You do jes' what I tell you and them walls 'll fall so hard they'll make a hole in the ground." "Spill it," agrees Josh, and the schemes is un-schum.

'Take it or leave it, this crack army o' Joshua's don't do a damn thing but walk around that wall once a day for a week— Monday, Tuesday, Wednesday, Thursday, Friday, Saturday too. Jes' walk around, blowin' horns. On Sunday they walk around seven times and on the last go 'round, the way they blow on them horns is too bad, Jim. Sounds like a flock of steam-boats lost in a fog.

'Then every son-of-a-gun and his brother unhitches a hell of a whoop and—take it or leave it—that wall comes tumblin' down same as if it was trained. Dynamite couldn't a done it no better. The birds on the inside have been laffin' at Joshua for a week—damn fool tryin' to blow a wall down, tootin' a few horns. The brass-band army. Huh—but now they ain't even got time to pull up their pants, and what happens to their hinies is a sad, sad story, no lie.'

But Shine did not repeat what Tod Bruce said from this point on. Enough to admit that you'd been in a church, without further confessing a genuine interest in the meaning of a sermon— especially if the meaning was a little too deep for you anyhow.

Bruce spoke quietly, without show but with impassioned conviction, and though many of his hearers no more grasped his message than did Shine, there was none who felt the same when Bruce ended as when he began. His honesty and sincerity were contagious and the very defects in his imperfect analogy revealed a convincing absence of artifice, a contempt for trifling disparities, an impressive disregard of minor obstacles in conveying a major idea.

'Many a man laughs,' said he, his voice penetrating like his eyes, 'at the preposterousness of this Hebrew fairy-tale. Some of you perhaps are laughing now. For your sake I am going to say something that a minister of the Gospel is not expected to say. I am going to say this: that I don't care the least little bit whether this thing ever happened or not. To us it does not matter. Consider it a Jewish legend—a parable of Paradise, if you will—a myth, without any basis of factual truth. Even so, the spiritual value of the story looms and remains tremendous.

'You, my friend, are Joshua. You have advanced through a life of battle. Your enemies have fallen before you. On you march till a certain day that sooner or later comes to us all. And then you find yourself face to face with a solid blank wall—a wall beyond which lies the only goal that matters—the land of promise.

'Do you know what that goal is? It is the knowledge of man's own self. Do you know what that blank wall is? It is the self-il-lusion which circumstance has thrown around a man's own self. And so he thinks himself a giant when in reality he is a child, or considers himself a weakling when truly he is strong, or more often judges himself the one or the other when he is actually both. There are still subtler contrasts: he may consider himself irreligious when at heart he is devout. Atheists and agnostics—this may be heresy, but it's true—are likely to be the most profoundly religious of all men, and clergymen, with whom it is all so routine, the least. A man may think he is black when he is white; boast that he is evil and merciless and hard when all this is but a crust, shielding and hiding a spirit that is kindly, compassionate, and gentle; may pledge himself to a religion when he is by nature a pagan, thus robbing himself and his generation of all that might come out of honest self-expression.

'There is no better advice, I think, than that of the ruffian on the street, whose motto is "Don't kid yourself". But we can't help kidding ourselves sometimes, and we almost always kid ourselves about our Self. And what is our Self, our knowledge of ourself, if not Jericho—chief city of every man's spiritual

Canaan? And how can we strip off illusion and take possession of our own soul save by battle? No man knows himself till he comes to an impasse; to some strange set of conditions that reveals to him his ignorance of the workings of his spirit; to some disrupting impact that shatters the wall of self-illusion. This, I believe, is the greatest spiritual battle of a man's life, the battle with his own idea of himself.

'Far more incredible than this tale of the Israelite warrior are the circumstances under which you and I engage in a similar battle today. It is easier to believe, I think, that the blast of rams' horns and the shouting of a mob could cause a stone wall to crumble than that you and I should hope to find ourselves—to take our Jericho—by some brief event that shatters in a moment what self-deception has built up only over the course of years. But it is true. It is not only possible—it must happen to all who would see things as they are. Self-revelation is the supreme experience, the chief victory, of a man's life. In all the realm of the spirit, in all the Canaan of the soul, no conquest yields so miraculous a reward.

'I urge you therefore to besiege yourselves; to take honest Counsel with the little fraction of God, of Truth, that dwells in us all. To follow the counsel of that Truth and beset the wall of self-deception. So will towering illusion tumble. So will you straightaway enter triumphant into the promised land.'

CHAPTER XVII

A CASUAL VISITOR to Seventh Avenue that bright Sunday noontime might have thought, on seeing the released congregations, that many had already entered triumphant into the promised land.

This weekly promenade is characterized not only by an extravagant and competitive elegance but also by an all-pervading air of criticism. Hither come self-satisfied, vari-coloured flocks from every fold in Harlem, to mingle and browse, to inspect and sniff, to display and observe and censure.

It must be explained that of Manhattan's two most famous streets, neither Broadway nor Fifth Avenue reaches Harlem in proper guise. Fifth Avenue reverts to a jungle trail, trod almost exclusively by primitive man; while Broadway, seeing its fellow's fate, veers off to the west as it travels north, avoiding the dark kingdom from afar. A futile dodge, since the continued westward spread of the kingdom threatens to force the sidestepping Broadway any moment into the Hudson; but, for the present, successful escape.

And so Seventh Avenue, most versatile of thoroughfares, becomes Harlem's Broadway during the week and its Fifth Avenue on Sunday; remains for six days a walk for deliberate shoppers, a lane for tumultuous traffic, the avenue of a thousand enterprises and the scene of a thousand hair-breadth escapes; remains for six nights a carnival, bright with the lights of theatres and night clubs, alive with darting cabs, with couples moving from house party to cabaret, with loiterers idling and ogling on the kerb, with music wafted from mysterious sources, with gay talk and loud African laughter. Then comes Sunday, and for a few hours Seventh Avenue becomes the highway to heaven; reflects that air of quiet, satisfied self-righteousness peculiar to chronic churchgoers. Indeed, even Fifth Avenue on Easter never quite attains to this; practice makes perfect, and Harlem's Seventh Avenue boasts fifty-two Easters a year.

Shine and Linda, released from church with the others, might have overheard much critical comment as they walked along Seventh Avenue:

'My Gawd. Did you see that hat?'

'Hot you, baby—!'

'—'Course it's a home-made dress—can't you see that crooked hem?'

'Wonder where the fire sale was?'

'What is these young folks comin' to—that gal's dress ain't nothin' but a sash!'

'Now you know a man that black ain't got no business in no white linen suit—'

But Shine and Linda had issues of their own to decide.

'How'd you like it?' she asked.

'He's a smart guy, that dude,' Shine passed judgment. 'After he got through tellin' 'bout that bird, Joshua, I didn't know what the—what it was all about. Where's he get that stuff 'bout knowin' yourself? How's a guy go'n' help knowin' hisself? What's the grand secret?'

'It's easy,' said Linda. 'S'pose a girl thinks she likes a fellow. Likes him better than anyone else. Then s'pose somebody else comes along and she falls head over heels in love with *him*. Well, see? She didn't know herself the first time.'

He grinned. 'Who was the guy ahead o' me?'

And she answered with merry eyes, 'There wasn't any. You're the first one. I'm talking 'bout the one that'll come next.'

'Hope I don't have to spank nobody 'bout you,' he said gravely.

'You make me tired,' she declared. 'Just because you're big, you've got the idea that nobody can lick you. You think muscle's everything.'

'It's all that ever done me any good.'

'*Did.*'

'I mean did.'

'Well, why don't you say what you mean?'

'Aw right—listen. Here's what I mean. I ain't never yet hurt nobody as much as I could've, see? But, what I mean, the first bird gets in between me and my girl—'

'Oh—you didn't tell me you had a girl.'

'Well I have—and she's the owl's—feathers.'

'Really?'

'No lie. She's right, what I mean. All 'cept one thing.'

'Yes?'

'Yea. She looks like an angel, but talk about one evermore hard woman to get along with—'

'I am not!'

'Who's talkin' 'bout you? Girl I mean ain't nothin' like you. This girl likes to go to church a lot and it's near 'bout ruined her. She's just as evil and tight and hard to get along with as all the other church folks.'

'That isn't true!'

'What isn't?'

'That about church folks. They're the best peoples on earth. Kind and nice and—everything. They're the only ones that even make believe doin' to others as they'd have others do to them.'

'Make believe is right. Look at my landlady. My landlady lives in church—all day Sunday and most every night in the week. Yea. But jes' let me miss a week's room rent—jes' one, that's all.'

'Is she the girl you were talking about?'

'Girl! Shuh—that woman's got a grandson in the old men's home.'

'Do you mean you don't believe in church?'

'Ain't talkin' about church. Talkin' 'bout folks. 'Tain't the church that makes the folks, it's the folks that makes the church. Only trouble with church is, folks ain't no 'count. All time kiddin' themselves, jes' like the man said this mornin'. He's right. Take my girl. My girl kids herself sump'm terrible. She thinks she's the hardheartedest Hannah that ever poured water on a drownin' man. But she ain't. Naw. Say, she's soft as a baby.'

'Is that so?'

'Yea. She ain't foolin' nobody but herself. Say—that's what that guy meant, huh?'

Linda sniffed and changed the subject. 'I'm going to change my job.'

'No!'

'Uh-huh. Got a new job starting next week—pays twenty dollars a week.'

'Pretty good for a girl. Y'know I always wonder how come you ain't in some show. Make lots more money.'

'Never tried—haven't had a chance. I was in the Home till I was sixteen and I've been in service these other two years.'

'Well you're lucky. Where you go'n' work now?'

'Right on the same street. For a man named Merrit.'

'Merrit?'

'He's a jig.'

'Don't do it.'

'What?'

'I said don't do it.'

'Why not?'

'Well, I know that bird. I done—I did a job for him once. He's funny.'

'What's wrong with him?'

'First thing is, he's a jig. Jigs is bad to work for.'

'*He* isn't. He's a—'

'Nex' thing he's too doggone yellow. Yellow men ain't no good.'

'No good! Huh—he's got money enough to—'

'Next thing is, he's a big-time dickty. Dickties is evil—don't never trust no dickty.'

'Well—is that all?'

'No. Worst thing is, he drinks too much liquor.'

'Really?'

'Patmore was crazy to get his trade a while back—claimed it was enough by itself to support him. I don't think you ought to have no liquor-head for a boss.'

'Huh! I can take care of myself.'

'Maybe. But where you're at now, you don't have to take care o' yourself. Th' extra money ain't worth th' extra worry.'

They had turned west, leaving Seventh Avenue, and were now entering progressively quieter neighbourhoods.

'But I've got to take it. I talked with his housekeeper, and she said I could probably go to night school 'n' everything. In a little while I could get a job in an office.'

'And turn dickty.'

'Well, you don't think I want to be a K.M. all my life?'

'I don't mean you to be. I'm go'n' have my own business one these days. Long distance movin'. Good money.'

'Really?'

The sarcasm was ignored. 'You won't have to be nobody's K.M. then.'

'You mean nobody else's.'

'Well, jes' since you get what I mean.'

'Well, I don't. And even if I did I'd take that job.'

'Why?'

'Because if I do I'll learn to typewrite.'

'You sure are the hard-headest woman—'

'Hush—and if I learn to typewrite you can give me a job in your office—when you get one.'

In astonishment he stopped to stare at her. The expression of mingled amusement, decision and tenderness with which she returned his look gave him a sudden overwhelming happiness. It almost upset him.

'Gee!' he said, his face shining. 'Gee—Lindy—'

He had an impulse to catch her up and kiss her right there on the street corner, oblivious to broad daylight and possible observation. Had he done so, spontaneously, on the crest of that emotional wave, the result would doubtless have been different. But the old habit of hardness, which for the instant he had almost escaped, promptly clamped itself down on his exuberance and distorted his natural impulse into a presumably safer substitute. Every act must be sentimentally airtight. The device he adopted to make this one so, lost for them both that surging moment to which the girl would have responded.

'Ain't it somewhere in the Bible sump'm 'bout turnin' th' other cheek?'

Puzzled, her own spell broken, she answered: 'You mean—if a man smite you on one cheek, turn him the other also?'

Before she sensed his intention, he had pinioned her arms and kissed her on one cheek. 'Well, turn me th' other one, then,' he grinned.

But Linda could play as safe as he. For answer she snatched herself away, and the sounding smack that met his face must have made the girl's palm burn.

Shocked, strangely hurt within, gigantically helpless without, Shine stood rubbing his cheek and watching her stride indignantly away.

What he eventually said was:

'Now ain't she a hell of a Christian?'

WALLS

CHAPTER XVIII

ON THE NIGHT when Shine told Jinx and Bubber the story of the battle of Jericho, he had no sooner left Pat's than another argument was on. Hitherto, Jinx and Bubber's nocturnal enmity had always ended at least without catastrophe; tonight catastrophe descended upon them, and the thing which each sought to divert by the very extravagance of his quarrel was by the same extravagance rendered inevitable. Tonight they came to blows.

Jinx started it.

'There now, you dumb Oscar,' he said to Bubber with great relish, in a voice that carried throughout Pat's bar room.

'There now what, jackass?'

'Didn't I tell you?'

'You ain't told me nothin'—and if you did, 'twasn't nothin' nohow.'

'I told you—' Jinx spaced his words for emphasis, 'that next thing we knowed she'd have 'im goin' in the main door of the church—and what did you say? "Aw no. Ain't no gal go'n' do nothin' like that to *that* boogy. Hard boogy, he is." That's what you said. Yea. And look. He comes in and tells us ev'rythin' the damn preacher said. Don't leave out nothin'.'

'That don't prove he went in d' main door,' argued Bubber with overacted patience. 'He could 'a' come down through d' skylight for all I know.'

'Like a big black angel, I s'pose?' said Jinx and grinned with surrounding laughter.

'Yea—or a long-legged, speckle-face giraffe,' retorted Bubber, swelling.

Jinx grew sombre. 'That's d' trouble with a li'l round black hippo like you. All give and no take. When you kid me I can take it. When I kid you you can't.'

'You don't seem to be takin' that so good,' said Bubber. 'Don't nobody get no madder 'n you do.'

'No? Look at you now. 'Bout to bust open and spatter d' whole bar room with ink.'

'I can remember,' Bubber returned, 'when you didn't act like nobody's long lost brother. Never will forget that night you got so mad you started slippin' me in d' dozens.'

This was approaching dangerous ground, this reference to their own reactions. To quarrel over subjects in general was bad enough; to quarrel over each other might be disastrous. It brought them closer to the truth about themselves, yet not quite close enough; it did not reach the actual sore, it only lifted off the scab.

'Well you oughta been slipped,' Jinx said. 'Any bird can't take kiddin' no better 'n that needs to be kidded and kidded hard.'

The customary comments accompanied this discourse:

'Tell 'em 'bout it!'

'That means fight in my home.'

'Grease us twice!'

'They jes' foolin'. If they meant it they'd both be dead by now.'

'Me, I'm bettin' on Long Boy. He'll wrap hisself 'round Squatty and squeeze all th' ambition outta him.'

Bubber challenged: 'Well—you better not slip me again.'

'No?' said Jinx like a small boy who has been dared to knock off the chip. 'No? Well—yo' granddaddy was a mule. Now—what you got to say 'bout that?'

Bubber said nothing. Instead he moved toward Jinx with surprising ease and mysterious rapidity and suddenly Jinx doubled forward from the force of an almost invisible blow to the midriff. 'What *you* go'n' say 'bout *that*?' Bubber asked, looking belligerently up into Jinx's astounded face.

Not quite certain whether this was serious or make-believe, Jinx reached mechanically forward and gathered Bubber's neck and shoulders in an embrace usually reserved for pianos. Failing to twist himself free, Bubber began swinging away at the other's kidneys, and in a moment the tussle removed from the atmosphere all suggestion of possible jest.

'Look at yeh!' somebody gasped.

'They ain't roughin' sure nuff, is they?'

'They ain't playin' hop-scotch.'

'Well, ain't this sump'm?'

But before either could damage the other, Pat, who was an excellent manager and always at the spot that needed him most, had heard the commotion from the next room and hurried to the scene. Pat was not bad with his hands himself, and it is significant that with apparent ease he managed quickly to separate them.

'What the hell you think this is?' he inquired, as for a moment they stood off from each other glaring.

'Jes' get out d' way, that's all,' said one.

'He been cryin' fo' it—now he go'n' get it,' vowed the other.

'Not here he ain't,' Pat decided. 'Look,' he pointed. 'Y'all see that door? All right. I told you once before, the next time you wanted to settle sump'm I was go'n' put you in the cellar and let the best man come up.' He strode to the door, unlocked and opened it, and pressed a button. 'Come on, if you mean it—come on.'

Neither was willing to admit that he did not mean it, and in another moment the gaping bystanders saw them disappear through the cellar door, which Pat promptly closed behind them.

'Well, what do you know 'bout that?'

'Ain't this a dog?'

'Salty dog, I mean.'

'Damn if d' worm ain't turned.'

'Yea—but which one is d' worm?'

* * *

The bystanders crowded about the door, listening. Pat, grinning, kept his hand on the knob, his ear against the panel. The others pressed forward: a lean black boy as tall as Pat, with tight slick skin and wide, white, shifting eyes; a thin, short tan-skinned lad of twenty, with a sharp face half hidden by a voluminous, lopsided cap; a paunchy old brown fellow in shirt sleeves and suspenders, with puffed cheeks and rolling pop-eyes; a long, thin, senilely crouching grandad with the complexion of a mummy and a gloating, toothless grin; a parchment-covered gambler, a tea-coloured card-shark, a khaki-skinned pick-pocket easing one hand into a pompous racing-man's pocket, a dozen others, all surging forward, all listening with arched brows or grins of relish. This was gonna be good, this was. Them two guys meant blood.

Most of these, hearing nothing, presently fell back commenting:

'Bet on the long boy!'

'Give you odds.'

'Don't tell *me*—that jasper can *fight*.'

'Squatty'll wear him down, though.'

'I knowed they'd ask for each other sooner or later—'

'Too bad now.'

'That's the reason I never kid nobody—might have to *make* him take it, see?'

'Wonder if they'll cut?'

'Can't tell what a guy'll do when he's losin'.'

'Who'll move pianos tomorrow?'

'Better get yo' mop out, Pat.'

'Anybody sent for the ambulance?'

'Ain't got a chance in the world—'

'Five bucks says he *is*—'

'Who—String-bean?'

'Put yo' money where yo' mouth is—'

It seemed an endless time, but nobody's eyes left the door for long. Stories suggested by the present affair began to be told, sudden gusts and flurries of laughter swept the room.

Argument ensued over the nature of the quarrel: How had it begun? So? The hell it had—it was like this. Good thing—those two were a constant pain in the what's-a-name with their continuous quarrel. Over a woman, hey? Huh—jes' goes to show you—

Pat was called away from his post by some duty in the pool room. He made sure the cellar door was locked and went about his business, promising to return in time for the rest of the fun.

Another long wait followed. 'Hear anything? Not a damn thing. Fools must have gone down there and killed each other. Remember the night Sam Tyler and Joe West got hooked up? Yea. Waitin', they was, in the same hotel. The head waiter give Sam a check that should have been Joe's, so Joe was sore to start with. Well the man ordered Washington pie, see? You know—that white stuff with whooped cream all over it. And Sam brought *chocolate* pie by mistake. So the fay man looked up at Sam, he did, and turned up his nose, like, and says, 'Waiter, I ordered George. You've brought me Booker.' Well, Joe heard it and when he got through kiddin' Sam about it, 'twasn't nothin' left for 'em to do but fight. Brother, I mean, neither one of 'em ever got over that scrap. Judas Priest—it's been three-quarters of an hour! Nary a sound. Better get Pat—thought he was coming back so soon? He was, but he got in a argument with Boody Mullins over a protection-fee. Well, let's go get him for Chris'sake—them two damn fools may be tricklin' all over the floor by now . . .

Patmore came hurriedly in from the pool room, flanked by the two who'd summoned him. He paused a moment to listen, his ear against the door. 'I hear sump'm,' he said. 'Wonder is—?' and at once unlocked and opened the door.

Everyone had pressed forward behind Pat, but now they all fell back, and as a lane opened through their midst, Jinx was seen framed in the doorway. He was swaying a little from side to side even though he attempted to steady himself against the door frame, and there was a far-off vacancy in his eyes that made him seem completely unaware of those who stood and stared at him. No one said anything, no one moved to help him, as he relinquished his support and started uncertainly forward.

He took four or five grotesque tottering steps, then his legs and feet seemed to get all tangled like those of a fly trying to escape sticky paper, and rather slowly he sank to the floor and lay crumpled in a twisted, senseless heap.

Pat, who alone of all the onlookers could afford to take an active hand in this matter, started toward that crumpled heap. A sound behind him brought him up short and he turned with the others to see the short broad form of Bubber come into and through the doorway.

Bubber looked decidedly dazed, yet not so much as had Jinx, and the unsteadiness of his bearing was somewhat modified by his rotundity. His progress through the crowd toward his prone enemy resembled that of a pool ball through a scattered field of its fellows, kissing first this one then that and accordingly zig-zagging forward from side to side, like the other balls, his fellows each withdrew a little at each glancing impact, not one extending a supporting hand or revealing a sympathetic impulse. Even Pat did not offer to catch him when he reached Jinx's figure, tripped over Jinx's feet, and fell across Jinx's body.

Then curious things happened.

Jinx, roused by the jolt of Bubber's fall, stirred drowsily with a movement that rolled Bubber off to one side, and Bubber was heard to murmur stupidly: 'Ain't nothin' to fight about, boogy. Ain't you my boy?'

Pat called abruptly to a bystander for help, and together they reached down and raised Jinx to his feet. He opened his eyes for a moment, then, as if realizing the futility of trying to see anything, allowed his heavy lids to drop again. They got him on to a chair and his head sagged limply forward.

As they were in the act of turning to render similar assistance to Bubber, something halted them half-about and they exchanged puzzled and apprehensive looks. Everyone exchanged similar glances with his neighbour, gazed at Jinx's sagging form in a fear that grew into conviction; for in that moment the something happened again, as if to substantiate itself by repetition: a shudder took hold on Jinx's body, shook it from below upwards, halted in his throat with a little choking sound that seemed almost to break his neck.

'Death rattle—Jesus—!' somebody muttered. One or two peripheral observers near the door eased stealthily out. 'Ain't go'n' be no witness in no murder case, no *sir*.'

Scowling, Pat stepped forward, seized Jinx's shoulder, shook him, called him, pushed up his lids with a thumb. Each lid, released, drooped slowly resolutely shut. Pat frisked Jinx's clothing, palpated him, searched swiftly but futilely for the wound that must have been dealt, swung around to find Bubber on hands and knees trying to rise, laid hold and yanked him to his feet. Bubber stood teetering like an exercising-ball, stared sleepily about, said: 'Where-my-boy?' and unceremoniously sat down unanswered. Pat strode through the cellar door and disappeared down the stairs.

Somebody now searched Bubber for a weapon, and somebody else said Pat had gone to find it. Periodically a spasmodic shudder almost jerked Jinx off his chair. Nobody seemed to know what to do, everyone was helpless.

'Must a strangled 'im, huh?'

'Seem like it—chokes off his breath.'

'Jes' goes to show you—'

Presently, Pat returned and came into the circle with ominous deliberateness. He stood for a moment looking down on the helpless pair, nodding his head in mingled conviction and disgust. Then he held up what he had found downstairs, a round quart bottle with perhaps a half-inch of whiskey left in its bottom.

'Give it to Jinx,' urged a bystander. 'Might stop that rattle yet—'

'Rattle, hell,' said Pat. 'That jigaboo ain't got a thing but the hiccups.' He set the bottle on the bar counter with a sarcastic thump. 'That,' he growled glumly, 'is the only damn thing they hit. They found a case.'

CHAPTER XIX

THE FACT that Linda had taken the job in Fred Merrit's house as soon as it was available seemed to Shine, like the slap, a mere gesture of defiance, as a matter of fact rather complimentary and encouraging. But the fact that she stubbornly withheld her company and had done so now for two weeks seemed an unnecessary emphasis of her already defined position.

And because it was for him an entirely new experience, for which his knowledge of women contained no therapy, his own futile resentment rendered him daily more and more violent. He worked harder and played harder and knew that nothing ailed him; but with a stubbornness greater than Linda's he refused to admit to himself that the girl had anything at all to do with the change. No mamma in this man's world was tight enough to put it on *him*.

Bess, the great van, became a willing mistress, and from her he derived a sort of unconfessed consolation; took to driving her at top speed whenever conditions permitted: when traffic was light and fast and Bess was empty; literally hurled her, roaring like a fire truck, along Seventh Avenue's asphalt; and when opportunity presented, took her over to the Speedway for a rattling headlong romp. On such occasions if Jinx and Bubber were present, they would exchange wise looks and apprehensive grimaces, and Bubber invited annihilation one day when, on narrowly missing a coal truck, he asserted that it just wasn't good arithmetic for no three men to commit suicide over one woman.

But the zest with which Shine drove Bess did not give him sufficient relief, left him still unsatisfied, like the deep but ineffectual breathing of a man suffering acute air-hunger. Hence his whole behaviour took on a reckless vehemence, and whether he laughed or cursed, worked, drank or gambled, he did so to excess.

Ordinarily he used two belts around an upright piano to be hoisted; two belts surrounding the treacherous instrument near either lateral end, a cable joining either belt to a central metal ring. When the tackle was hooked into this ring and raised, the two short cables became the legs of an isosceles triangle, the apex of which was the ring and the base the top of the piano. This arrangement was absolutely proof against tilting and slipping.

Now however he decided, just for meanness, to dispense with approximately half of this apparatus and used only a single belt about the middle of the piano. It pleased him then to stand off and dare the blam-blam thing to slip.

Ordinarily when he drank it was with a modicum of caution. No sense getting drunk down. The way to lick liquor was to hit it and run—no man was lined with copper. Drop in on one of these new young doctors that had to write 'scrips' to make it; or go to one of these drugstores that had prescriptions already written and could sell you the best rye right off at five or six bucks a pint. On thirty-five bucks you wouldn't be able to do that but once a week, and so you'd be pretty sure to take it easy.

Now, however, he told himself he could drink anything anybody else could drink, and drink as much of it, too; sought out the vendors of synthetic corn and gin and drowned himself in the pale stuff; and cursed to find that he awoke the mornings afterward without even so much as a headache.

Ordinarily, when he played blackjack in Pat's back room, he played with a definite system: started with the minimum stake, doubled three rounds, then passed. Above all he never hit seventeen.

Now he played with no regard for rules or the laws of chance; doubled often five times straight, 'stopped' the bank at every opportunity, and invariably hit a soft seventeen and usually a hard one as well.

None of these devices satisfied. Not a piano slipped, none of the liquor proved to be poison, and at the end of a week his blackjack stood him eighty-six berries to the good.

In the midst of these exaggerated reflexes, an order came to the office of Isaacs' Transportation Company for the removal of one load of valuable furniture from Fred Merrit's country house to his residence on Court Avenue. Old man Isaacs was off duty, ill abed with a bad heart, otherwise Shine would have had the boss appoint a new foreman. Finding this impossible, he told himself that no girl's presence was going to make him dodge a job any damn how.

There was, nevertheless, an unmistakable reluctance in his piloting of Bess this morning. Merrit's place was only a dozen miles north of New York, but it took Bess two hours to get there. Once arrived, there was much palaver about the best way to negotiate the terrain.

'This place just sprawls all over this hill,' observed Bubber. 'Looks like a flock o' hen-coops. How we go'n' get up yonder?'

The question was settled by uproarious but careful navigation of a steep side road which led to a plateau behind the flock of hen-coops. Here they were greeted by Mrs Arabella Fuller, who began at once to wheeze interminable directions.

Eventually, in spite of all Mrs Fuller said, the load was on, each piece swaddled partly in quilting, and partly in that lady's verbiage, which seemed to hover about it long after Bess was headed back townward:

'Yes—that goes—that's a picture of his mother—the only one he's got, so be awful careful. I know he'd die if he lost it. Take care o' that if you lose all the rest. Now be careful—y'all never care how you handle things and them table legs'll snap off if you sneeze at 'em. That's a genuine redwood table and you know them's expensive—look out for that vase! The way y'all handle things, anybody'd know they wasn't yourn. Child, that vase cost more 'n yo' foot—if it break yo' foot yo' foot'll get well, but if yo' foot break *it*—yes—them's chests and you needn't

think they ain't valuable and that you can scrape 'em up bad
as you please jes' 'cause they ain't got no paint on 'em and got
the hinges on th' outside; they come from Siam or some them
places Mr Fred was where the folks is all coloured but won't
admit it and you carry 'em by puttin' two broomsticks through
the sides, but 'deed I ain't got no broomsticks for y'all to scratch
up and break—they have their own kings and queens and
ev'rything jes' like in the Bible, only I say coloured folks ain't
got no business tryin' to act white 'cause it always gets 'em into
trouble. Where's that other boy—that big one come with y'all?
Why don't he turn in and help? He's big enough—ought to be
ashamed o' hisself letting y'all do all the work. Ain't we been
had the worst summer, rainin' every day and look like it always
had to catch me outdoors with nothin' on my head and you
know what happens to this kind o' hair when it gets wet—'

'Whew-ee!' heaved Bubber. 'Damn if that woman can't talk
d' spots off d' dice.'

'No lie. I ain't got my breath back yet—jes' listenin' to her.'

'Yea—and you tellin' her she could ride back with us if she
wanted.'

'Who?'

'You?'

'When?'

'Didn't you stop and tell her to come on, let's go—we was
finished?'

'Oh yea. But I swear I thought I was talkin' to you. Y'all look
like sisters. If you and her didn't have the same granddaddy,
somebody played a awful dirty joke on you both.'

The inevitable quarrel ensued, and this somewhat took their
minds off Bess's unusual jogtrot. If the trip out had been slow,
the trip back was endless. For out of all that had reached his
ears, Shine remembered only one part of Arabella Fuller's dysp-
noeic discourse, and this hummed in his mind as persistent
and unvarying as the rumble of Bess's innards:

'Go where, child? Back to town with y'all? 'Deed I'll have

to stay out here almost another week packin' things for the winter. Y'all go right ahead, though—Linda's there and I done told 'er where to tell y'all to put ev'rything—'

Linda living alone in the house with Fred Merrit, toper and dickty.

A piano is a malicious thing, the temporary dwelling of some evil spirit that follows you from one instrument to the next. Sooner or later that spirit catches you off guard and, using the instrument as its weapon, swiftly, viciously strikes. Either it gets you then and there or is itself permanently defeated.

Every man who enters this work thereby invites this pursuit. Both Jinx and Bubber had escaped for a time, but finally each had been caught. Bubber had lost a part of one foot. Jinx's elbow had been crushed, leaving a permanent deformity. These injuries, however, did not materially hamper their work, and so Jinx and Bubber considered themselves fortunate; for, as the superstition had it, they now enjoyed immunity.

Shine had so far gone without a scratch, had never been caught off guard. It was Jinx and Bubber's belief that he would probably go on escaping. What chance did any piano have at a steel man lined with cast-iron? Shine was just as hard toward things as toward people, no more vulnerable in the one case than the other, and though ordinarily he could afford to be more generous and genial than most men, who dared not thus risk imposition, still in a pinch he was known to be more unyielding than bedrock. Nothing fazed Shine. 'Remember how he held on to that piano the day the roof broke?'

But today for the first time Shine's preoccupation put him quite off guard; and so today his evil pursuer struck.

The piano was an elderly upright which Merrit kept because it had been his first luxury. It was to go to the front room on the third floor of the house, a room which had been set apart as a remote and private playground—a combination of den, poker room and too-bad-party resort. The instrument stood alone and sullen at the edge of the cluttered sidewalk, aloof, superior, apart, permitting the lesser pieces to go first.

Shine, likewise aloof and apart, refused to enter the house with the others. He saw Linda only once, when first she gave Jinx admittance, and although he did not allow himself to make frank observations, he was aware from many a covert glance that the girl had withdrawn into the inner regions, evidently as intent upon avoiding him as was he upon avoiding her.

The time soon came, however, when all but the piano had been removed. Shine's active participation had so far consisted only in handing things down from the van. Now he must direct the hoisting and so lend a more active hand.

It was now that his brooding inadvertence combined with his recently assumed recklessness to make him do an unprecedented thing. During his two years of working with Jinx and Bubber he had not once trusted either of them to anchor hoisting tackle. But now, instead of going to the roof of the house to anchor the tackle himself, he ordered Bubber to do so in his place. He'd be damned if Linda should think he was trying to see her.

'Well—what the hell's holding you?' he inquired as Bubber hesitated, doubting that he had heard aright. Bubber turned slowly, shaking his head and meditating aloud:

'When that boogy gets evil he gets *so* evil. There's so damn much of 'im.'

'Then come down and unsash that window,' Shine commanded balefully, 'and stand by to pull in, see?'

Jinx would have followed to check up on his confrère's technique, but Shine halted him to give further orders.

'You keep them flat feet of yours right on the sidewalk and hold on to this guide rope. I'll do the pullin'. When Squatty pulls in up there you can go up and help him take it down.'

So it was arranged, and presently Bubber, directed to the roof by the red-hottest mamma that had ever smiled upon him, was casting about for anchorage. A cylindrical airduct presented itself as the most likely object to use: it was well away from the front ledge of the roof, giving good purchase, it was of ample height and diameter, and it was apparently constructed of heavy cast-iron, cold, black, and shiny. As a matter of fact it was made of glazed mortar and had a hidden joint just below the roof.

To this duct Bubber made his major attachments, using many windings of line and an intricate system of knots; and for double security he carried the line ten feet further rearward to a chimney and around this wound the rest of it, fastening it uncompromisingly with a second complex of knots. When he tossed his tackle line over the edge, it was with the air of one who is sure that at least *his* end of the job has been well done.

Shine, on the sidewalk, had surrounded the uncovered piano with a girdle of quilting, and about this, somewhat loosely, had adjusted a single belt. Now he hooked the block into a ring fastened to the top of this belt. Then, with quite unnecessary vigour, he took hold and began yanking on the pulley. Jinx held the guide rope. The piano began to rise.

It rose in a succession of small, upward jerks, each epitomizing the vehement force that Shine imparted to the pulley line. That force, increased by the piano's weight, extended to the anchorage on the roof, and the joint of the airduct in the floor of the roof felt and responded to each impulse from Joshua Jones' inner conflict, heard and answered each wanton effort to vent through muscle what could not escape through mind. An even ascent that joint might have borne, a jerky one it could not; there was no question of whether it would snap, but simply of when.

Shine's malevolent pursuer chose to decide this important question: the piano was just short of the end of its journey when the break came. Shine, getting a sort of satisfaction out of prodigious effort, gave an especially tremendous tug—to find resistance vanish so suddenly that he pitched forward on his face still holding the line. He heard Jinx utter a terrified 'Jesus!' and as he rolled over, instinctively attempting to clear the pathway of the falling instrument, he glimpsed it swaying above, knew that a second 'safety' anchoring was all that gave him that instant's doubtful grace, and heard a girl scream, 'It's slipping out—! Quick—it's slipping out!'

The second anchorage held, but the initial drop had been enough to displace the soft girdle and belt from the centre toward one end of the instrument. There was an instant's hesitancy, as if to give direction, and abruptly the belt released the piano, which dropped like a live thing freed; plunged with a drive to crush and kill, like a beast pouncing on witless prey. The crash was like no other sound on earth—explosion, groan, and whine—thick wood, coarse metal, taut wires—a noise that struck and shattered itself, then rose, spread, and hovered. It was as if a corner of hell had been blasted off and a thousand souls swarmed out, wailing.

Shine stood erect, looking dazedly about, touching an abrasion over one eye with exploratory fingers. And miraculous as a vision, Linda was before him, breathless with horror, apprehension, relief, with the effort of reaching him so quickly.

'Honey—' she said, and found that nothing more would come.

'I'm all right. Gee—if you hadn't 'a' hollered—'

'Oh—' she managed, 'I was at the window—upstairs—' and stood there a while in silence. Then because words failed, because something pinioned her arms that wanted to reach out to him, and because her eyes and throat mysteriously and ridiculously filled, she had a blank moment in which to realize how silly and impetuous she was, and another in which to be ashamed and take swift refuge in the house.

Shine on one side, Jinx on the other, looked down upon the wreckage. The piano lay half supine in a grotesque angular posture, its row of white keys gleaming like teeth, the lid of its keyboard sprung back and fixed, like the retracted upper lip of a creature that has died in agony.

Jinx gave forth a prayer of thanksgiving:

'It sure as hell meant to get you—but it's long gone now.'

Shine remained silent and contemplative. Bubber came down. He and Jinx ejaculated comments. Bubber came over to palpate Shine and ask how the hell he ever missed it. A small crowd was gathering. People were looking out of windows.

'Crazy as hell,' Shine muttered absently. '"Honey—" Well, I'll be john-browned—' His hand again touched the raw place over his eye. 'Little cold water wouldn't do it no harm—'

And following in Linda's wake, he too entered the house.

CHAPTER XX

THAT SHINE should visit a hospital when he felt almost perfectly well meant that some decided difference had come about in him. The scramble which had delivered him from grave injury had had no more serious visible effect than to abrade his hands and forehead against the cement, but it marked a conscious internal change which first came to light when he followed Linda into the house. Shine, the disciple of hardness, would not in any imaginable situation have been guilty of a surrender like that. Now again the change appeared when he decided that maybe he'd better go on 'round to the man's clinic and let one them doctors look him over—might even be some bones broke, who could tell?

He sat at one end of a white metal pew, an article of hospital furniture as uncomfortable in fact as it is in suggestion, and awaited his turn. Funny kid, Linda. Come runnin' out there yesterday, scared clean white, then didn't do a damn thing but turn around and go back. But 'Honey—' Yea. He fell for that. And when he went in the house for water—huh—she was like as if nothing had happened. Showed him the sink and let him wash his head and gave him a towel—but not another word. Honey. Yea. When he had stalled around as long as he could, he too said: 'Well, honey—' And all she answered—didn't need to be so tight about it, either—was, 'You better go see a doctor and make sure you're all right.' Damned if he would. But here he was—a whole day late, but here.

Since Harlem Hospital was in a state of transition, it happened that, of the two interns on the service, one was white with brown angora goat-hair and the other brown with black sheep's wool. A blank white door opened, a patient was ejected and the white intern beckoned summarily to Shine. Shine looked at him a moment then said:

'I'll wait for th' other doctor.'

He settled back in his pew. Sweet kid, though, no lie. All women are funny, but you can overlook that—if they're good-looking enough. And Lindy was sure good to gaze on. Skin like honey—honey with red cherries in it. Clear like thin wax with light behind it. You could almost see through it—you could see through it—you could see red flowers behind it; and when she got excited over anything it seemed that somebody waved the flowers back and forth. Like in the Casino that night, or that Sunday on the corner of Court Avenue. Gee—! Eyes, too. Talk about eyes! Looking into her eyes was like looking into the sky at night—looking from the bottom of an airshaft: deep, soft and awfully black, with bright little stars twinkling a way off. That night on the Drive—Judas Priest!

'Next!' called the brown intern cheerfully from a different blank white door, and Shine found himself in a clinical dressing room with tables and screens about and a little bed on wheels in one corner. There were mysterious vari-coloured bottles and jars and wickedly gleaming instruments everywhere, and the odour of phenol and iodoform took all the humour out of the air.

Not, however, for the intern nor the dressing-nurse who assisted him, a little round, stiffly starched brown doll-baby who should have been in a toy-shop window.

'Yes, *sir*,' said the intern to the nurse, watching as she soaped and dried Shine's forehead. 'Best looking girl that's been in this place since the man said "Let's have Harlem". Came in last night late. Ward VII. I sure mean to see her again.'

'Ward VII. Oh Doctor—not Ward VII!'

'What difference does it make? She can be cured.'

'Find out her name?'

'I didn't miss. Young. Linda Young. And as soon as dressing clinic's over, the doctor—ahem!—is going to take Miss Linda's history. This fellow's my last case. Oh boy—how I love to take histories: Did you ever have measles, chicken-pox, whooping-cough, mumps, scarlet fever? How many children? Oh no—of course not—I meant brothers and sisters? How many nights a week do you have to yourself, and how? When were you last out with the boyfriend? And now you have a pain in the bottom of your stomach—?'

The intern dabbed iodine on the denuded area of Shine's forehead. An abrasion, baring the most sensitive nerve-ends, is nothing to dab iodine on without due consideration. But Shine might have been anaesthetized for all the pain he felt. Linda in this hospital? Linda? What the—? Linda?

The intern finished his dressing after a fashion and bustled the dazed Shine out, hurrying on past him. The intern was on the way to more pleasant duties.

Shine, numbly incredulous, followed slowly in the same direction. The white uniform was soon lost in a tangle of other white uniforms. Shine wandered on. Ward VII. Oh yes, you want the G.Y.N. service? Down that way, turn left then right ... Looking for some place, mister? Ward VII? Second floor north. Ward VII? Right around the corner—yes, you'll see the sign—if you look ...

Ward VII. Yes, this is Ward VII. Whom do you wish to see? Linda Young—yes, she's a new patient. Have you a card? She's a ward case you know, and visiting hours are over. I'm sorry, but you'll have to go back and get a card.

He went back to get a card. Miss Linda Young on Ward VII. Was it a relative? No. Just a friend? Sorry. Couldn't be issuing cards all day. Come at visiting hour tomorrow—two to three P.M. Very sorry, but it was really against the rules. Find out how she is for you, if you like. Click ... G.Y.N? ... How is Linda Young? ... Yes. Resting comfortably? ... Click. Resting comfortably.

Scarcely able to sense direction, Shine wandered away through a labyrinth of hallways. Linda resting comfortably— what kind of a joke, for Pete's sake? He was completely lost when, after a long time, he met a familiar figure, the intern who had dressed his wound and gone off to consult Linda Young.

He caught the intern by the arm—had a crazy impulse to laugh at the way in which the intern shrank from that apparent attack. The intern had quite forgotten him.

'Listen, doc. Linda Young—Ward VII—I want to know about her.'

'You want to know about her? 'Know what?'

'Is it really her?'

'Really her? What the—? Do you know her?'

'She—yea—I know her well.'

'Oh—so you're the guy?' There was untold scorn in the intern's voice.

'Me? What guy? Is she hurt?'

The intern looked him over cynically. 'You ought to know.'

'Know? Know what, doc? I didn't even know she was sick. I saw her yesterday. She was all right yesterday.'

'What time yesterday did you see her?'

'Early afternoon.'

'Early afternoon. Oh. Well—she came in late last night. You didn't see her last night?'

'No. Why? What's wrong with her?'

'Nothing much. Only some guy ought to get his block knocked off.'

'What you talkin' 'bout, doc?'

'Tell me—is this your girl?'

'She ain't nobody else's?'

'Well then, you ought to know this. Some guy found her alone last night where she works, see, and tried to—show her a deep point. He couldn't make her listen to reason, so he tried cave-man stuff. There was quite a scuffle. The girl got loose and out of the house, but she keeled over on the sidewalk before she got two blocks away. Scared dumb. She was brought in with a diagnosis of assault with intent—'

The change that distorted Shine's face told the intern he had gone far enough. The features writhed, the bronze skin seemed to have suddenly been dusted with ashes, and there was unquestionable intent to kill in his eyes and the whole attitude of his body. The intern, too late as he now realized, tried to mitigate his story:

'It's all right of course—he didn't succeed. She's just got a sprained ankle and a little shock—'

But Shine brushed past and moved away in huge, infuriated strides. Even far down the corridor he looked the size of ten men.

The intern watched him swing out of sight, then shrugged his shoulders helplessly. 'I wonder,' he asked himself, 'when I'll learn some sense?'

BATTLE

CHAPTER XXI

OVERNIGHT Fred Merrit's Court Avenue house had become a ghastly ruin. Every pane had been bashed in with flood, every window frame charred with fire, each of the grey stone window margins frayed and blackened with smoke. Yesterday, these windows had surveyed the world serenely, bright and alive. Today they looked like the deep, dark circled orbits of sunken blind eyes.

The place had been gutted, heart and bowels. Its vitals, whatever things had given it substance, circulation and life, all had been hopelessly battered and crushed till they'd shrunken out of sight. One could stand on the sidewalk and see the sunset through and beyond the rear wall—a hard broad grin of a sunset, which transilluminated the flame-sacked dwelling, mocking its emptiness without pity, deriding its devastation. When eventually the sun's grin faded out, it was as if a contemptuous, amused observer had at last turned aside and gone off on more important business. The house stood stark as a corpse in the shrouding dusk.

It was upon this scene that Shine came, less frantic now, but no less grim than when he had left the hospital earlier during the day. Even then he had realized that Merrit would not be found at home during the day, and had finished his afternoon's work in a silent turmoil. Added delay had not subdued his fury—had merely stored up a greater potential violence, like added tension on a spring. Now, when he unexpectedly came upon this ruin, it was as if the spring suddenly cracked.

He stood on the sidewalk looking up at the looming grey carcass of a house. For a moment it took his breath. Twilight made it the more indistinct—he craned his neck forward and stared; looked all about him to verify the neighbourhood, walked forward to a point where he could discern the number on the house next door—315—came back, stood in a stupor of unbelief, and after a while heaved a great sigh of reluctant, bitter conviction:

'Damn if the fays didn't get 'im,' he muttered. 'The dirty—' For the time being his present mission of vengeance was submerged in the onrush of a greater hatred, a hatred more deeply ingrained and of far longer standing; for the moment he glared insanely around at the cool, still, empty street and at the rows of serene grey houses standing side by side. They gave forth a maddening impression of distance and unconcern. They looked quite satisfied. This catastrophe was for them the answer to all their prayers. Now that it was done, they could go on as they always had. The ruined dwelling had simply earned and received the wages of sin. If Shine could have trampled and crushed them all in that moment, he would surely have done so.

But as this tide of hatred fell and receded, his original murderous intent emerged like a spire through abating flood. What if they had got Merrit? A guy like Merrit deserved everything he got. And he hadn't got half what was coming to him yet—not if he could be found—Linda resting comfortably— the dickty liquor-head—

He knew it. Merrit had meant to put it on her ever since that first morning here on Court Avenue—the morning she strode past like a million dollars, ignoring Jinx and Bubber's comments. 'Figurin' on a jive already—the doggone dickty hound. Why the hell can't dickties stick to their own women, instead o' messin' around some honest working girl?' That was the thought he had got from the way Merrit looked at her that morning. Well—it wouldn't be long now. Let him get one hand on that yellow throat; just let him sink the fingers of one hand into it; just let him take the bastard's ankle in his hands and twist it off—

But this house. Hell almighty—what a wreck—

His turbulent emotions strangely dominated by curiosity, he slowly—almost fearfully—made his way up the front stoop of the house. Shattered glass, strewn over the steps, crunched dryly under his feet. The doorways bounding the vestibule were open, the outer door a mere frame to which angular fragments of glass still clung like monstrous teeth; the inner a fallen barrier, shattered and blackened, prone on the floor.

He explored the front room, stepping cautiously over obstructing wreckage, just able to perceive in the dimness the utter, unsparing destruction; ceilings black, walls grey and water-soaked, woodwork a burnt-cork caricature, patches of plaster fallen away baring the carbonised understructure.

'Whoever done this sure knew his business—the—'

The floor was a clutter of water-soaked pieces, some still wrapped in burlap. A cabinet lay on its side in a corner, its upper half bared and blackened, its lower still embraced in a scorched, wet covering. Little puddles glistened here and there; a rug protested under Shine's step with the squish of a full sponge, compressed. A besooted prism-chandelier still hung from the channelled ceiling, against the grey of which it was silhouetted like a shadow of itself. To the rim of the broad doorway leading from this room there still hung traces of what had yesterday been portières of metal brocade, now shreds of grey lace woven of cobwebs, the greater part fallen about the threshold, a scum of soft wet ash.

'This ain't a damn thing compared to what I'll do to him—'

Shine moved through the foyer past a crumbled charcoal staircase, and on thence into the back room. This room, equally demolished, was narrower than the front, and presented at one side a doorless doorway leading into a small side room. Disregarding the settling darkness, Shine went over to this doorway, then suddenly halted, stood quite motionless, intent on an unexpected sight within that room.

The rear wall was almost entirely occupied by a tall broad

window. There was a table before this window, and seated at
the table, a man. Looking obliquely through the doorway, Shine
saw that the man did not sit wholly erect, but slumped down
in his chair as limply as if his backbone had melted, drooped
there almost double, his head bowed forward on his chest.
Despite this lifeless posture, it was possible to recognize the
figure by the grey dusk of the window against which it was
outlined. Shine knew that he was looking upon Fred Merrit.

He stared scowling a moment, bent forward a bit to catch
some sign of life, and was on the point of approaching the figure
when it moved in a curious way: shook like a man with a chill—
slumped quiet—violently shook again. Slowly it dawned on
Shine that maybe the bird was crying. And as he continued to
stare and wonder on this unfamiliar sight, he became aware of
something grasped in one of Merrit's extended hands: a fairly
large picture-frame, out of which the canvas had been burnt,
leaving only a frayed, singed, marginal rim. Shine belaboured
his brain to catch an elusive memory of that frame, till it broke
upon him that this was the one that had contained the likeness
of Merrit's mother; the one about which Mrs Fuller had warned,
'He'd die if he ever lost it.'

For what seemed a long time Shine stood looking, things
romping through his brain. Linda struggling—no—resting
comfortably. The Goddamned dickty—what happened? Fays
got him—dirty sneaks—I *mean* they got him. Look at this place.
Merrit. There he is—what the hell—crying—Jesus—that picture
of his mother—

Then Shine did what would have seemed to his associates
an amazing, an unpardonable thing. There with the man he'd
set out to punish alone, within his grasp, he stood silent, apparently undecided, made not a single move to strike. And after a
while, slowly turned about and found his way out of the house.

It amazed Shine himself—amazed him and chagrined him.
He felt rather glad of the darkness outside—it was a sort of
balm for his shame. Hard boogy he was—yea—awful hard—the

hardest boogy in Harlem. There he was, this dickty, this guy that—right there, crying to be crowned. And what does the hard guy do—the hardest boogy in Harlem? He gets a seasick feeling in the belly and turns around and sneaks out!

He mumbled excuses to himself as he wandered away down the street:

'Hell—I'll get him later. Gee—you can't hit a guy when he's down—'

CHAPTER XXII

HE WAS the first visitor to arrive on Ward VII the next afternoon. The odour of phenol and iodoform that had pervaded the clinic hovered here also. The beds were repellently white and orderly. There were only a few scattered patients—ugly women in bath robes and mules.

He found Linda seated beside a bed. A profusion of cotton and gauze was piled at one end of the bed. From these Linda—with great concentration and delicate, mysterious precision—was fashioning oblong pads which she stacked at the opposite end. Her back was toward him, and he stood for a moment behind her, looking; and if yesterday he had had strange emotions watching the unaware Merrit, today his feelings were past understanding watching the unaware Linda. Nothing seemed to be wrong with her, yet the sight of her sitting there in that clean, sparse, terrible place, bending so intently over her task, made his breath stop in his throat, so that he had to swallow it deliberately before he could speak.

'Hello, Lindy.'

She turned and looked up, half rose, sank back; the stars came out in her eyes, which consumed him in unbelieving astonishment, and she gave a little catching laugh. 'Why—how'd you know I was here?'

He appropriated the chair beside the next bed and sat down.

'Didn't you tell me to go to the hospital?'

She quickly sought the iodine-stained place on his forehead, reached impulsively toward it, checked the motion. 'No—'tisn't s'posed to be touched, is it?'

'You—all right, Lindy?'

'Great. Going home today. Wasn't any sense in them bringing me here anyhow. I wasn't—I was only scared—I guess.'

'That all?'

'Well, I hurt my ankle—see?' She displayed a bandaged joint. 'Not bad. Strapped. They'd transfer me to another ward if I wasn't leaving so soon. How'd you know?'

'Doc in the clinic told me. Told me all about it.' There was silence. To relieve her embarrassment, evident by her averted face, he assured her, 'He won't pull nothin' like that any more, Lindy.'

She was alarmed.

'You didn't—didn't—?'

'Nope. Not yet.'

'Don't!'

'Don' t? Don't what?'

'Don't—you know. It's all right. Really. You'll get into trouble—'

'Trouble?'

'Please—'

'Listen, baby. Trouble ain't half what I'd get into if—'

'But what's the use? What good will it do?'

'He's got it comin' to him.'

'He'll get it—without you gettin' into trouble.'

'I ain't go'n' get in no trouble. It's him that's go'n' get in trouble.'

She was silently distressed, and this reinforced his vengefulness as if he were witnessing her original pain instead of this that he himself was causing. He too was silent, far in the depths of a thwarted and now redoubled malevolence. Just let him get his hands on that half-white dickty cake-eater—he'd tear him apart slowly—he'd rip his yellow arms out. Just let him get that close again—

But the vision of Merrit as he'd last seen him, limp and shuddering amid devastation, grew clear, whereupon, in spite of himself, this redoubled malevolence sagged.

Linda said: 'Remember that morning in church what Father Tod said 'bout Joshua and the battle of Jericho? 'Bout people kidding themselves?'

'Yea. I can see that story all right 'bout the walls; that's a good one. And I can see how people kid themselves. That's easy. But I never did get the connection. Little too deep for me.'

'You're the connection.'

'Me?'

'Uh-huh. There's a wall around you. A thick stone wall. You're outside, looking. You think you see yourself. You don't. You only see the wall. Hard guy—that's the wall. Never give in, never turn loose. Always get the other guy. That's the wall.'

'Mean you don't really believe I'm go'n' get this bird for what he done to you—?'

'No—no—no. He didn't do anything. I mean—'

'Gee, Lindy—what'd you think of a guy that claim to be likin' you and let a bird get away with anything like that?'

'He didn't get away with anything, I keep telling you.'

'He didn't miss trying.'

'I'm not talking about just him. I mean all the time. Everything. You're kidding yourself. You're not hard.'

'What?' His eyes dilated as if that explicit remark were a sort of doom.

'You're not hard or mean or tough or any of those things. You're just scared.'

'Scared?'

'Scared. Scared to admit you're not hard. Scared you'll be found out. So scared, you take every chance you can to prove how hard you are. I don't believe you'd ever do anything really cruel. Don't believe it's in you.'

Again that vision of Merrit stricken and of himself paralysed, strangely unable to strike. Linda kept on:

'You're just big. You can lick everybody. So you get away with it. All you have to do is let folks think you're hard. That's all right. Let them think so if that's any fun. But when you think so yourself—well, you're kidding yourself, that's all.'

He grasped vaguely for comprehension and captured only excuse:

'Well, you kid yourself too sometimes, Lindy.'

That seemed to kindle something in her that flared and persisted like fire. 'I know it—and I'll never be happy while I do. Oh, I see what he meant all right. I tell myself things, things about you. I tell myself I don't even want to see you any more—that you can't be really liking me after I let you pick me up. Yes, that's what it was, a pick-up—that night in Manhattan Casino. I tell myself I hate you for grabbing me up on the street that Sunday. Lies—all of 'em. I liked it. I've been wild to see you. And the only thing I hate about you is the thing that keeps you from telling me what I'd give both ears to hear. But no—you wouldn't do that, because'—her voice was all scorn—'just because you're hard and it's soft to fall for a girl.' Her eyes filled, and she turned her face away, biting her lip.

To save his life, he could not utter a word.

'And now look at me,' she said, her face still averted. 'Making believe I'm ashamed when I'm not a doggone thing but mad. Oh you're right. I kid myself, too.' There was a long pause. Then, 'But I know I'm doing it. You don't.'

'But listen, Lindy. The only time I tried to tell you, you hauled off and bat me one.'

'Of course I did.'

'But now you're sayin' you liked it.'

'I didn't say I liked the way you did it. Playing safe. Making me quote the Bible—giving yourself protection. Scared. Scared to be yourself. That's what I—that's what I hit at.'

For a while there seemed to be nothing to say. When at last Shine spoke, it was to make a quite irrelevant statement:

'Lindy—I'm crazy 'bout you.'

Still she did not look at him, but she said:

'That's how I know about you. That's how I know you're not really hard. That's why I don't want you to bother—him. You say you'd be doing it for me—but you could kill him and it wouldn't give me any satisfaction—just make me unhappy because you'd done it and kept us apart—maybe for life. So if you bother him now, knowing I don't want you to, knowing it won't give me any satisfaction and it will only make me unhappy, why then you'll just be doing it for your *own* satisfaction. You'll just be proving again to yourself how tough and tight you are. It won't be because you're crazy about me—that'll just be the excuse.'

He went through a good deal of figuring before he answered that. What he eventually said was:

'Well—I'm crazy 'bout you, Linda.'

Only then did she look fully at him, and again there were stars in her eyes, and colour deep in the honey of her skin. She gave him that little halting laugh and said: 'The walls must be tumblin' down.'

He wanted to tell her then about Merrit—how right she was. He wanted to tell her how completely she had dominated him these past days, all the newly realized illusion about himself that now was crumbling. He wanted to say, 'Walls? Tumblin'? You said it, baby,' but habit sealed his lips.

It did not however close all avenues of communication. He reached out, not fully aware of his gesture and placed his great hand over hers on the bed. She placed her other hand on top of his. It was the closing of a switch, the making of a circuit through which leaped new, strange, shattering impulses. Not a thousand dances all in one with Lottie Buttsby could have moved him so, not a thousand of Babe Merrimac's entreaties and frank admissions. For one brief, eternal moment that mere contact of hands completely obliterated the surroundings, as if their whole bodies had been fused in passionate, tender embrace. When eventually the white beds came back into the picture, they might have been billowy clouds, the ugly women in their bathrobes and mules might have been winged angels, and the odours of phenol and iodoform might have been the fragrance of roses.

Shine smiled. He thought yet again of his strange behaviour yesterday which now through her, he was beginning to understand; and the self-disgust he had felt as he spared and left

Merrit within his ruin began curiously to give way to a sense of tremendous relief.

A familiar sound came from outside. Bess had been parked in the street below. Jinx and Bubber had grown impatient and were 'laying' on the horn, by way of suggesting that the driver hurry and return. The sound came faint but clear through the open windows.

'Know what that is?' Shine asked her.

She smiled and answered: 'I guess that must be the ram's horn.'

CHAPTER XXIII

IN THE small back room of Pat's place, the regular evening blackjack game was in session. A green shaded electric light hung low over an oval dining-room table covered with a dishonourably discharged brown army blanket. Around it a dozen players sat and around them a dozen side-betters stood. The room was full of men and smoke and low talk.

The dealer, standing, taunted the players in a soft, half plaintive voice:

'What's your contribution, friend? Only a half? Can't buy the sweet mamma shoes on four-bit bets. How much to you, dumb-and-ugly? One buck, right. Next? A dollar and a dime to Jinx, the freckle-face wonder—dimes for luck—my luck. How about you, Squatty? Make it light on y'self. Two-dollar bills is bad luck, you know. What d'you say, Stud? The rest of it? Nineteen bucks four bits to you. Deal it? Consider it doled. Perfect, gentlemen, perfect.'

He had dealt each player a card as he spoke. Now he dealt them each another, renoting the amounts of their bets as the second card fell. He put down the rest of the deck, picked up his own two cards and, holding them close to his chest to prevent his neighbours seeing them, studied them long and hard. Suddenly he warned with exaggerated malignancy: 'Don't a man move! Knew I'd turn the bug on you dinkies this time!' And he threw down an ace and a jack, the supreme combination.

He was collecting his winnings when Shine came in, edging sidewise through the crowd. Finding no place available at the table, Shine would have ordinarily lifted some player out by the collar, thanked him with a grin, and assumed his place. Tonight he simply looked on. Had anyone else appropriated

valuable space just to look on without betting, there would
have been trouble. First gentle hints about how crowded it
was, then less gentle hints about the value of fresh air to
kibitzers, and finally, if the offender was especially dense, an
ultimatum suggesting that he try the pool room or the roof.
Nobody, however, manifested a trace of annoyance at Shine's
profitless presence.

As for Shine, he felt tonight a new exhilaration, a satisfying
ability to fill his lungs, a conscious, pitying superiority over
these companions of his. For to him, through Linda and after
considerable meditation, had come a new outlook on old
things. He had finally been able to phrase it for himself in
terms that brought it home to him, terms that made it ridiculous to feel shame for having let Merrit off unpunished. He
put it thus:

'The guy that's really hard is the guy that's hard enough to
be soft.'

That about got it. That covered him. That made him unafraid
to do what he damned pleased in any situation. If he felt like
letting a bird off, he was big enough to do it. Hitherto he'd
been like a little shrimp that dares not go without a gun or a
knife, only his size and strength had taken the place of the
weapon. Sort of coward, sure enough—no wonder it made
Lindy sore. She sure had got him told, too. Sure had—some
kid, no lie. Funny he never could see it before—the walls of
Jericho. Lindy—Judas Priest—he'd forgotten to ask where she
was going from the hospital. Dumbbell. Well he'd find out. Gee,
what a feeling! Boy! Like a port-wine drunk—

He saw the me 'round about anew: lean and long bodies,
thick and short, round heads, egg heads, bullet heads, steeple
heads, thick lips stuck out, thin lips drawn in, skins black,
brown, tan, yellow. He picked out two or three strangers,
conjectured about their occupations. This lopsided one was
undoubtedly a waiter; that plump cocoa one a porter; the
bald, custard one whose cheeks had been left in the oven a

trifle too long, a—well, what the hell else were boogys but waiters and porters?

In this superior frame of mind, he was not at all prepared for what he was now to learn.

Wearying of the turn of cards, the stereotyped comments of players, the occasional deft, furtive exchanges between collaborating cheaters, Shine waded out into the pool room, where the air was a trifle less thick. Here the talk was loud and the laughter unmuffled; the clack and clatter of pool balls, the thump of cue sticks, the eager shuffle of players' feet freed this room of the covert atmosphere oppressing the other.

As Shine abandoned the game room he encountered Patmore who was coming toward it; and he was a little surprised to observe Patmore quite so drunk. A slick coat of sweat made Pat's face shine as though it had been greased; his eyes also were unusually bright and his manner a trifle too genial.

'Hello, Mr Jones!' he greeted Shine. 'What's Mr Jones gonna say tonight?' And Shine felt a vague disproportionate annoyance at the ironic form of address. He brushed past with a noncommittal response, while Pat stood back, turned to watch him pass, and grinned derisively: 'Must be turnin' dickty.'

Shine ignored this as he had ignored Pat himself ever since the dance. He found a cue stick and an empty table and proceeded to amuse himself solitaire. He had hardly racked-'em-up when Bubber appeared at his side.

'Come 'ere,' Bubber said, 'Come listen to this.' And Joshua Jones went and listened.

Pat was proclaiming to all his friends in the game room:

'Yessir. Fair and square, that's Henry Patmore. Anything you do for him, he's gonna do for you. Good or bad, don't make no difference. You know what the man says—as ye sow so shall ye reap. You see me go—I'll see you go. You put it on me, I'll put it on you. Sooner or later. Don't make no difference—sooner or later, that's all. Five years ago, I tell you, this dickty—dickty, mind you—put it on me, see? Cost me damn near all I had. Ten thousand Goddamn dollars. Cost me that to stay out o' jail. Yessir—ten thousand berries. Well—that's aw right. Jes' go up on Court Avenue and look at his house now. Huh. Thought I'd forgot it, see? So damn smart, movin' in 'mongst d' fays. Fay nigger. Movin' in 'mongst d' white folks. Well, d' white folks sure give 'im a welcome. Jes' go up on Court Avenue and see what d' white folks done. White folks. Yea. Henry Patmore— white folks. Hah! Damn if this ain't d' first time in my life I ever passed for white.'

The players were giving Patmore only divided attention. They had heard such proclamations before, and no particular example of any of Pat's special excellences could be expected wholly to detract them from their game. But at this moment the dealer, who was still standing, caught sight of Shine looming in the doorway; and the dealer became fixed as suddenly as a figure in a cinema when the projector abruptly stops; fixed in the act of dealing, with his thumb at his lip and the deck in his hand, his eyes wide, set, unmoving.

All the men turned and looked. What they saw affected them differently. The dealer, now like an actor in a slow motion picture, his eyes still set on Shine, put the deck down on the table, gathered up the bank without looking at it, and retreated toward the far door of the room, which led into the saloon. Those nearest him seized their piles and moved in the same direction, as if the dealer were attached to them, drawing them along by strings. The lopsided waiter backed terrified against the wall and stood there as if stuck, while the plump cocoa porter, his eyes on Shine, clawed absently and futilely at the place on the blanket where his pile should have been, and made no effort to rise. Some pushed back their chairs and yet seemed too fascinated to get out of them, some jumped up and elbowed their way through the midst of their slowly retreating comrades, while a few sat quite still as if aware that the effort to get clear of danger was useless. All this because of what even the blindest of them saw in the face of Shine.

Not slowly, first with doubt, then with mounting conviction, had revelation come to Shine this time; not as in the case of the ruined house, nor of the sobbing Merrit, nor of Linda's analysis of his hardness. Not so, but instantaneously, like something revealed by lightning in the dark—the moment he heard Patmore's words he knew all of what had happened; knew who had craftily sent Merrit that fake warning the day before the lawyer moved in; knew who had thus established an alibi, awaiting an opportune moment to strike safely when suspicion would fall elsewhere. Knew who, finding Linda alone, had renewed the advances which had been interrupted at the Manhattan Casino dance; knew all Pat's motives and all his moves, from the unsuccessful attempt months ago to enlist his own aid as an 'agent' to this last vicious spiteful snap at him himself, through Linda. And it seemed that all the hatred he had ever felt for anybody welled up within him to be concentrated now on Henry Patmore alone: his hatred of the asylum superintendent, of the fay who had called him Shine, of all fays, of the evil thing he'd escaped in pianos, of dickties in general and the blameless dickty Merrit in particular—all these now gathered in one single wave, advanced in one tidal onrush. And all that he knew and felt gleamed in his bronze face.

Patmore saw it there and confessed everything by reaching for his gun. Jinx, one of those who had not moved from his seat at the table, was near enough to strike at Pat's arm as the weapon went off. Shine felt his left hand go numb, felt his hatred break into action. All of a sudden he became a madman with no notion of what he was doing, with no sustained consciousness, only a succession of fragments that thumped in his head.

Linda resting comfortably. Merrit crying like a baby. Picture of his mother. Fays sure got him. Fays? Fays hell—Patmore got 'im. Wonder how many kinds of a jackass that guy thinks I am—? Never seen a man catch air so fast. Walls tumblin'—damn if they ain't. Offered me twenty-five dollars—no—Linda. Fly guy, passing for white. Assault with intent—not Merrit— Patmore. Patmore done it—did it. Not the fays—Patmore. Patmore put it on Merrit. Like *this*. Walls—haw! Damn right, walls—look at 'em fall—let 'em raise hell when they fall—like that Goddamn piano—

From the saloon room a few observers, some of them those who'd escaped the game room but had no intention of sacrificing the spectacle of a good fight, watched the tumult grow. The game room door had been shut tight behind them, but the wide passage between the saloon and the pool parlour revealed a part view of the latter; and presently forms came into sight, were framed in the doorway, vanished, returned for brief moments. The field of vision was maddeningly small, but it showed that more men than Pat and Shine had become involved in the battle. Those who watched could not know that when Jinx had knocked Pat's gun out of line, an adjacent friend of Pat's had seized Jinx and retaliatively yanked him back, that Bubber had cheerfully kicked the shins of an other interferer who would otherwise have tripped Shine at his first move; an interferer who resented interference and so promptly turned on Bubber; that from such small beginnings the conflict had grown to a come-one-come-all fracas, and that Jinx and Bubber were gleefully trouncing some of those who would have enjoyed seeing them trounce each other not long since.

Unintelligible, fragmentary glimpses came through the too narrow doorway—Bubber ducking a cue stick swung butt-end-to in a villainous arc—somebody reaching for a pool ball, in a corner of the one visible table—a figure pitching forward headlong out of sight—Jinx with a pianohold vehemently bending his particular adversary back across the edge of the table—wild swings of bodiless arms, senseless twist and tangle of disjoined legs and feet. Accompanying these glimpses was noise, a strident yet muffled tumult: shuffle of feet, grunts, curses, thumps, thwacks, hisses, stifled cries; a deep background of sound against which stood out an occasional wooden crash.

And now there swept into the doorway, framed as if by stage design, that pair of antagonists from whom all the others derived their energies, the two whose bitterness reduced the rest of the conflict to mere friendly tiff. Patmore, ordinarily no mean combatant, now gin-mighty and frantic with fright; and Shine, a gigantic madman, himself heedless of what everyone else saw: that his useless left hand was an impediment to himself and a decided advantage to Pat, a more than equalizing damage and all that had prolonged the battle.

They had lost their coats and clawed each other's shirts into shreds, and though Pat had been shiny at first, he now glistened no more than Shine. Shine however, maintaining himself with one arm, gave the superior impression: blocked knee-jabs, anticipated kicks, foiled elbow-thrusts, invalidated all the other man's rough-and-tumble skill. Even in the short time and brief space of this doorway view, one could see that all of Pat's effort was maximum, final, as though he were trusting each blow to be decisive; while Shine's every move only anticipated some future stroke that he knew would be wholly crushing. Every instant, every buffet seemed to enlargen his ominous intent; his purpose mounted visibly, so that those who watched saw in him not merely one crippled yet splendid in battle, but a towering, inescapable instrument of vengeance.

The end came suddenly. Had Pat been less of a toper and less of a jiver, it might have been different, but in a prolonged encounter these handicaps of his were far more telling than Shine's. A thrust from the latter's bare left shoulder sent Pat's head back like a blow from a fist. It snapped away the last of his reserve, and all of a sudden his whole body sagged as if his spine were broken. Clinging to Shine like a man slipping down a tree trunk, he sank to the floor on his knees, and his head remained sprung back like the open lid of a box. This was the moment that Shine had seemed to be awaiting; his fist hip-high, he deliberately drew back his right arm to strike the exposed throat. Every observer knew that if that blow should land, Pat's neck would be broken.

It did not land. Some friend of Pat's in the room beyond hurled a pool ball at the imminent victor. The heavy ivory sphere missed its mark, sped through the doorway and over the observers' heads, shattering the great bar mirror behind them.

The crash and jangle of the falling glass wall was all that snatched Shine out of madness. The sound transfixed him as if all the walls of the place had tumbled instead of just one. He stood set, motionless, blinked once or twice and stared a long moment at Pat.

Only then, perhaps, did he actually see him, on his knees, gasping, helpless. Presently the poised, retracted arm began to relax; the tension went out of Shine's frame. His head sank a little forward, and his good arm slowly dropped to his side, as limp as its useless fellow.

JERICHO

CHAPTER XXIV

WHENEVER a caller told Fred Merrit an unanticipated story, he whirled about in his swivel chair, jumped up and walked to the window. This he did now, as soon as Shine stopped talking. For a long time he stood looking down on the Avenue.

'Well,' he said at last, 'I'll be tarred and feathered if that isn't the damnedest—'

His office commanded a corner. On the kerb, two portly well-dressed idlers stood in leisurely conversation; they proclaimed their important opinions to all and sundry. A thin, hunched, hungry-eyed vagabond nearby watched them in ominous silence. A boy with yellow hair and the fairest of skin came slowly up the street, leading an aged, black, grey-bearded blind beggar.

'Can you imagine it? A Negro—using white prejudice to cover what he wanted to do—putting the blame in the most likely spot—almost getting away with it, too. Can you beat that?'

Merrit came back, sat down in his chair and shook his head. 'So it wasn't Miss Cramp after all. I swear I thought it was she. Well—' he showed himself true to his race hate—'it isn't because she wouldn't have done it if she could.' He banged his fist on the desk. 'I'd bet the insurance on that house that Patmore just beat her to it.'

'Insurance?'

'Yes sir.'

'Mean the house had life insurance on it?'

Merrit laughed. 'Yes. Not a bad name for it.'

'Mean you didn't lose nothin'?'

'Well, not as much as you'd think to look at the place.'

'Well—but when I seen you in there—'

'Yes—I know. I had been out of town overnight—just got

back that afternoon. It was quite a shock—but it wasn't the house. Not altogether. That is—the picture, you see, wasn't insured—can't replace that.'

'That's too bad,' said Shine.

'Got to admit he was wise,' Merrit mused. 'Sent several of those warnings. Wise. Rather admire that chap really. And I swear I'm sorry it wasn't the fays.'

'Well—' Shine rose—'jes' thought you'd like to know the whole story.'

'Wait a minute—where you going?'

'Goin' to look for a job,' Shine grinned. 'Old man Isaacs bumped off this time. Business for sale.'

'Sit down. Let's have a drink.' Merrit produced part of a pint and they drank, rat and dickty, as equals.

The drink gave Merrit a thought:

'You know what killed old man what's-his-name? Your boss?'

'Bad heart.'

'Yea. And bad news: when he heard you busted my piano. You're a hell of a mover.'

'No lie,' Shine admitted. 'But the next guy won't know nothin' about that.'

'Yes, he will.'

'Huh?'

'Keep your jumper on. I'm the next guy.'

'Say, it gets you quick, don't it?'

'What?'

'The liquor.'

'I'll be on my feet when they haul you out, my boy. This isn't whiskey talk. Listen.'

Shine listened. He owed Merrit a piano, so it was to Merrit's advantage to get him employed. On the other hand, Merrit owed him—or the girl, maybe—something more. Nothing but the grace of God had stayed Shine's hand the evening he stood behind him, intent on murder. All right. Here was the idea: Here was a business. Shine knew that business, didn't he? Been in it five years now. Why the hell couldn't he run it, then? He ran it when the old man was sick, didn't he? Suppose Merrit bought it—easy—only a one-truck moving business—and turned it over to Shine to run? Fifty-fifty on the profits with an option to purchase outright in due time. That's what we Negroes need, a business class, an economic backbone. What kind of a social structure can anybody have with nothing but the extremes—bootblacks on one end and doctors on the other? Nothing in between. No substance. Everybody wants to quit waiting tables and start writing prescriptions right away. Well, here's a chance for you and a good investment for me. Race proposition, too. How 'bout it?

Shine had no word to say, so suddenly had this thing come.

'All you put up is experience,' Merrit said. 'You've got your own hoisting licence, haven't you? You and that girl can hit it off sooner, maybe—she's out to the country-place now, by the way. And there you are. Well, what's the hold-up? How about it?'

Even now that Shine saw Merrit meant it, all he could manage to utter was 'Gee—!'

CHAPTER XXV

THE THRILL and terror of a house afire so uncomfortably close by had been a little too much for Miss Agatha Cramp. Even now, a week after the night of the uproar, she was still having breakfast in bed. Every time she thought of the excitement—the smoke, filling the quiet neighbourhood before anyone suspected its origin, the long wait for the engines while the flames gained headway, the shriek, roar and clangour of arriving fire trucks, men shouting, thumping her own front door, yelling for admittance, dragging hose line through her house to the roof—she had to suppress shudders and draw deep breaths. It was a shattering ordeal.

She said as much this morning over her tray to her new Irish maid, Mary. Mary, an extremely acquiescent person, answered solidly: 'Yes 'm.'

'I feel so badly,' Miss Cramp went on, 'about such a great loss of property. It must be extremely discouraging. The poor man never had a chance to take up his residence in the place, you know.'

'No, mum.'

'No. You see, he was a Negro.'

'Yes 'm.'

'And I shouldn't be surprised if someone weren't guilty of arson in this case.'

'Y' nivver kin tell, mum,' said Mary wondering what in limbo arson was.

'There is so much hatred between races,' sighed Miss Cramp. 'Still, it is all that can be expected. Now Negroes, for instance, are most extremely deceitful.'

'Is 'at so, mum?'

'Indeed it is. Why, this man Merrit, who owned the house

that burnt up, he was always practising some sort of deceit. Do you know what he did, Mary?'

'No, mum.'

'Of course you don't. Well, he was extremely fair of skin, you see, so that you wouldn't ordinarily have noticed that there was anything wrong about him. So many generations in this climate, you understand. But he was always posing as a white man.'

'Y' don't say, mum.'

'He certainly was. He posed as white when he purchased that house—otherwise he'd never have gotten it. And, Mary, you can't imagine what else he did.'

'No, mum.'

'He even went so far as to deceive white women in order to get into their homes—God knows for what purpose.'

'Is that so, mum?'

'Yes. So you see, after all, some disaster like this was all that he could expect. It was simply poetic justice, that's all.'

'Justice of the peace,' amended Mary.

'I once had a coloured maid. She was very deceitful, also.'

'Is that so, mum?'

'Very. She used to go out at night without letting me know, and finally she left on only three days' notice.'

'Y' don't say, mum.'

'So you see, everything considered, there is some basis for race-distrust after all.'

'Like England and Ireland,' suggested Mary.

'Exactly, Mary. Exactly what I was thinking. And that reminds rne, Mary.'

'Yes 'm.'

'Who is the president of your country now?'

'Feller named Coolidge,' said Mary.

'No, no, Mary. I do not mean the United States. I mean the Irish Republic, your native land.'

'I sorter fergit, mum,' Mary apologized. 'Y' see, when I come away, sure there wasn't no Irish Republic.'

'Isn't it a man named De Valera?'

'Yes—I believe it is, mum.'

'Now there is something I can't understand: how a Spaniard—
he is a Spaniard isn't he?—how a Spaniard could become a
native son of Ireland?'

'Well,' said Mary philosophically, 'them things will happen,
mum.'

'But I wonder, Mary—I wonder if your people don't need
help. Look at the way that McReeny starved to death. Something
ought to be done. Isn't there some organization that takes care
of such matters?'

'I think his family buried him all right,' Mary reassured her.

'No—no, Mary. You do not understand at all. What I mean
is this. Here is a young and inexperienced newborn nation,
planted on a little isle of the sea, and left quite alone, helpless.
It does seem to me that those of us who are in a position to do
so should contribute all we can toward their welfare.'

'Yes 'm.'

'Indeed there should be some organization having that as its
purpose. Are you sure there isn't?'

'Well—there's what they call the Irish Free State Association,
mum.'

'There!' said Miss Cramp triumphantly. 'I knew it. Exactly
what I thought, Mary. I must get in touch with them at once.
Have they a 'phone, do you suppose?'

'Wouldn't be surprised if they did, mum.'

'Very well, then. That will do, Mary. That's all. When you
come for the tray, bring the 'phone book, will you, Mary?'

CHAPTER XXVI

WHEN SHINE, en route upstairs with Bess, drew up at the driveway that led into Merrit's country-place, he had no idea that the sound of Bess's voice would awaken even the dog. It was barely daybreak, and though Merrit had promised yesterday to be up in time to greet him as he passed, Shine had no faith in the possibility of getting a dicky out of bed in the cool grey dawn. It surprised him therefore to see, before a minute had elapsed, a dim figure at the head of the driveway coming quickly toward him.

It surprised him a good deal more, however, when the figure came near enough for recognition. It was Linda, bareheaded, wrapped in a coat, smiling at his astonishment.

'Heard you were coming,' she said. 'Got up early and waited.'

It seemed to Shine that the sky turned from grey to gold in the twinkling of an eye.

'When you coming back?' she asked.

'Tonight.'

'Tonight?'

'Yea. Barrin' accident. Only a fifty-mile trip. Got to go pick up a load and bring it back.'

'Where's your gang?'

'Still getting over the fight—I'll pick up a couple o' guys to load on up there.'

'And you'll only be gone till tonight?'

'Be back by bedtime easy.'

'And you're going up alone and coming back alone?'

'Sure.'

Linda made up her impetuous mind. 'You're doing no such thing, Mr Jones.' And she circled Bess's nose and clambered into the cab from the opposite side. While Shine regained his

167

breath, she casually adjusted herself; stretched out her legs, rested her head back, hunched up her coat, stifled a yawn and murmured with great unconcern:

"'S chilly—huh?"

Merrit from the head of his driveway had seen her climb into the cab. Before he reached the road, Bess, with a joyous roar, carried them off. Too amazed to call out, Merrit went on down, out into the middle of the road, and having confirmed his vision, grinned and told the world he'd be damned.

He stood there smiling and watching in the middle of the road, one hand absently plucking at his throat where the soft, open collar of his shirt left it bare. He had preposterous feelings, far too absurd to admit: an impulse to run after the departing Bess, crying, 'Wait—for God's sake—' as if she were carrying off some chance of his own; a terrifying sense of some slow crushing futility, allowing them to escape, but holding him captive, surrounding, insulating, oppressing him, like the haze of this morning's mist, beyond which he could perceive but out of which he could not emerge; as if he moved and must always move in a dismal, broad, grey cloud, outside of which were clear blue skies that he could know of but never reach.

Strangely irrelevant people and things flashed into and out of his mind: a fleeting glimpse of his brown mother's picture; Patmore in court shaking his fist; Tod Bruce in his pulpit drawing some remote and ridiculous analogy; Shine in the office explaining unintelligibly why he 'let him out'; Miss Cramp inviting him to call. Why in hell couldn't it have been Miss Cramp instead of Patmore? All wrong, the way it actually happened. Should have been Miss Cramp. Should have been the fays—damn it—fays were supposed to do such things. Well, of course, Patmore had just beaten 'em to it—just beaten 'em to it, that was all. Bright boogy, Patmore, figuring it all out like that—bright jigwalker—knew how to do things. Perfect alibi—perfect . . . Jigs had a future, really—jigs were inherently smart . . .

He stood and watched and smiled. The road led up and over a crest beyond which spread sunrise like a promise. Away for a time, then up moved Bess, straight into the kindling sky. With distance, the engine roar grew dim and the van seemed to stand and shrink. Against that far background of light he saw it hang black and still a moment—then drop abruptly out of vision, into another land.

THE END

ONE MONTH'S WAGES

THE PUBLICATION in 1928 of *The Walls of Jericho* helped to cement Dr Rudolph Fisher's reputation as one of the more successful writers of the Harlem Renaissance. He had already published numerous short stories dealing with Black culture in urban America, and would go on to write one more novel, *The Conjure-Man Dies* (1932), which has the distinction of being the earliest Black detective novel published in book form. As well as the same sharp wit and social commentary, the book featured other elements from *The Walls of Jericho*, most notably the comic duo Jinx Jenkins and Bubber Brown, who get deeply embroiled in the murder mystery. Although Fisher's plans for more novels were cut short by his untimely death, he did revisit Jinx and Bubber in a short story, 'One Month's Wages', which finds them down on their luck in the early days of the Great Depression and desperate to find ways of raising some cash . . .

HENRY PATMORE'S POOL PARLOUR outflourished the green bay tree. Elsewhere depression might sweep Negro Harlem's businesses, subdue Eighth Avenue's turbulent markets, dim Seventh Avenue's bright theatres and speakeasies, chill Lenox Avenue's hot dives and nightclubs, but depression was a new broom that failed to find Patmore's corner. Here, occupying a reclaimed store on upper Fifth Avenue, in black Manhattan's backwoods, sat broad, stolid pool tables side by side in two long, level rows, each green tabletop illuminated by a low-hung shaded droplight. Between these tables countless players chalked their cue-tips, reached up to check off their scores overhead, squatted to diagnose the lay of the balls, or leaned far over table-ends to attempt long, difficult shots; big, yellow men in wide-striped silk shirts, short, scrawny black men in bright polo-jerseys, genial biscuit-brown fellows with slick bald heads, slim, wiry youngsters with patent-leather scalps, jests, gibes, laughter mingled with smoke, through which came the frequent thump-thump of cue-butts against the bare wooden floor, signalling the busy attendant to rack up a new game at so much per cue.

But Bubber Brown could not afford so much per cue tonight. A month of idleness had taught Bubber so much about depression that now he occupied free space on a long spectators' bench against one wall. Short, round, and of a complexion bordering on the invisible, he sat looking absently upon the prosperous scene, his customary grin absent, his hands folded before him in silent meditation. Stud Samson, Patmore's henchman, stopped in passing to comment on so unusual a pose:

'Boy, you look like a ebony billiken. If you hadn't blinked,

I'd 'a' picked you up and asked the boss how much. What you doin', son, repentin' yo' sins?'

Bubber grinned, revealing an absence of upper front teeth that lent his face a child-like innocence. 'I was jes' sittin' here wonderin' how old you was,' he said.

'Twenty-eight,' Samson told him, unsuspecting.

'Go on, boy,' scoffed Bubber, 'you couldn' 'a' got that ugly in no twenty-eight years.'

But further exchange of compliments was prevented by the arrival, at this juncture, of Bubber's friend of long standing, Jinx Jenkins, whom he had not seen for weeks. Unceremoniously he abandoned the scowling Stud and a moment later he and Jinx were greeting each other characteristically: halted a few feet apart and regarded each other in mock astonishment; whereupon one cried, 'No it ain't?' and the other avowed, 'Yes it is!' and both yelled, violently shaking hands, 'Well I'll be a monkey's uncle!'

They sought out a corner, 'Boy, where the hotel you been?' Bubber asked, 'I ain't had nobody to laff at for six weeks—'

Jinx was long, lean and lank, with freckled yellow skin and a habitually grumpish manner. 'I was runnin' on the boats, but me and the steward had a li'l argument 'bout a missin' lobster—'

'Seem like the steward didn' agree with you.'

'Lobster didn't 'gree with me, neither.'

'And me eatin' sawdust for cereal. What's yo' capital?'

'Three bucks.'

''Tain't 'nough.'

'You broke too?'

'You starin' Humpty-Dumpty in the face, boy. If somebody don' put me in a plaster cast, I'll be lopsided the rest o' my life.'

'Shuh. I was fig'rin' on puttin' up with you a while.'

'Try and put,' said Bubber. 'Know what the landlady say today? She say, "Look-a-hyeh, boy. Is you ever tried holdin' up a bank?" I say, "No'm. I'm honest." She say, "So'm I, but it ain't bringin' me nothin'. And a bank can stand a hold-up better 'n I can."'

'Signifyin',' growled Jinx.

'She's due to signify. I'm fo' weeks behind. And tonight's the night.'

'Couldn' we sneak in, 'thout her knowin'? If I could get to a real bed, I might sleep us up a idea.'

'Never no sneak in. That woman don' sleep long as anybody owe her a dollar.'

'Maybe we could jes' rough on past her?'

'Never no rough. She's a steam-roller woman. You get rough and she jes' smooths you out.'

'Looks like the park is beckonin' to us, don' it?'

'And us without no parkin' license.'

The extremity was genuine enough, as evidenced by the fact that they had foregone their usual derision of each other, a masquerade in which they customarily took the keenest delight. Each was the other's best friend on earth, but neither would have admitted the fact under torture. On the contrary, to Jinx anything Bubber did was wrong, while to Bubber whatever Jinx attempted was funny. So the scowls of the one and the grins of the other were the habitual outward expressions of what was no doubt great affection.

'Wait a minute,' said Jinx. 'Lemme think.'

'What thinkin' you do in a minute won' help.' Bubber looked on with growing apprehension while Jinx made faces over the problem. 'Give it up, boy,' he advised gently, 'befo' you hurt yo'self sho' 'nough.'

'I got three bucks,' mused Jinx.

'And two flat feet,' Bubber added helpfully

'Pat used to run a blackjack game.'

'Which,' Bubber reflected, 'is how come we so broke now.'

'A little luck would straighten us out.'

'So would a dose o' poison.'

Jinx reached his decision 'Don' take the poison till I come back. I'm go'n' try one mo' time.'

'It's yo' money,' Bubber said resignedly. He looked ruefully after his departing friend, who was already flailing a path through the pool-players toward Patmore's card-room in the rear. 'But three dollars worth o' ham and eggs is a lot o' grub to up and throw in the street.'

Nearby a pair of wags were mocking a friend. Their talk caught Bubber's interest; he looked and he listened.

'So you didn' get fired. You resigned,' said one.

'Yea,' derided the other. 'Imagine. Bread line at Times Square half a mile long. Doctors and lawyers blowin' their brains out. Bootleggers ridin' in flivvers. And you resigned.'

Their victim, a thin little nervous, jaundice-brown man, smiled a pale, wan smile.

'Couldn' stand it no longer, that's all. I ain't been well—and that work ain't healthy nohow.'

'Neither is starvation,' said the first. 'Quittin' a job in the middle o' hard times—jes' like jumpin' overboard in the middle of the ocean. I declare, I don' b'lieve you that dumb.'

'Dumbness,' the second agreed, 'is everybody's privilege, but it really ain't right to abuse it.'

Said the nervous one, '"Tain't dumb to look out for yo' health. I was 'twixt the devil and the deep blue ocean.'

'And had to choose both, like a hog—Better go on back to work.'

'Who—me?' The little fellow's uneasiness increased. 'I wouldn't go back to that job—' a haunted look dilated his eyes—'for the key to the United States Treasury. It's there for who wants it. I had enough.'

The critics desisted and went their way, leaving the ex-employee alone. Bubber approached and inquired:

'Brother, did you say you left a job unoccupied?'

The other confessed.

'Do the jug,' pursued Bubber, 'still crave a stopper?'

'Reckon it do. But you don' want no job like that.'

'Mean it's a freeby?'

'Oh, the pay is good, but—'

'Good pay un-buts it all, brother. I ain't lookin' for sump'm to like. I'm lookin' for sump'm to live on. Where is it?'

Still the little man hesitated. 'You sho' the kind o' work don' matter?'

'Mister, I'd dig a subway to China for six bits. Locate yo' job.'

'Well—twenty-three hundred Seventh Avenue. Ask for Mr Dade. Martin Dade.'

'Write it down and sign yo' name to it—you know—sort o' like a reference.'

The nervous one complied tremulously, woefully, as if he were being forced at the point of a gun to sign a friend's doom. Bubber, oblivious, grabbed the slip of paper and waved it like a banner of triumph:

'Red light, hard times!—If I ain't too late, funny-lookin', you gets a big box o' cigars.'

'I don' smoke,' said his strangely reluctant benefactor.

'I'll even smoke 'em for you,' Bubber promised brightly. 'So long.'

Out he hurried with the peculiar rolling gait to which bow-legs and pigeon toes predisposed him. His course lay westward, through a side street which, despite the late hour, was still alive with children running, yelling, and getting underfoot, and with grown-ups cluttering stoops and entrances—women nursing infants and scolding runaways, men huddled in white-shirted pow-wows, palavering over Babe Ruth or Kid Chocolate. Across the bright lights of Lenox Avenue he hastened and eventually into the splendour of Seventh.

Theatres had just let out and the sidewalks teemed with strollers. They were in no hurry and, it seemed, intentionally got in Bubber's way; tall bareheaded boys in bright-coloured sweaters and white trousers, bobbed-haired girls in voluminous flowered frocks. In and out amongst them dodged the plump and eager job-seeker, up lively Seventh Avenue, past drugstores, ice cream parlours, hot-dog stands, frozen custards machines, lunchrooms, gin-mills, cigar stores, and communistic stump-speakers excitedly urging black men to turn red. On toward Twenty-Three Hundred he hustled reading the house-numbers aloud as he made progress northward:

'Twenty-two eighty—twenty-two eighty-fo'—new hat, new suit—twenty-two ninety—new shoes, black ones with white stripes on 'em—twenty-two ninety-six—breakfast, lunch and dinner ev'y day—twenty-two ninety-eight—'

Suddenly he stopped in the middle of the sidewalk, staring dumbly at a single broad plate-glass window. In the centre of the window was the number he sought, a large unmistakable 2300. The crowd divided and passed him by. He looked about him in dismay, peered hopefully to either side of that plate-glass window—hopefully but in vain. There was no other 2300 save this, behind whose polished pane a gentle radiance illumined palms and ferns. Above the 2300, gleaming, sinister gilt letters announced: MARTIN DADE—and beneath the 2300 similar letters explained: UNDERTAKER AND EMBALMER.

The air hung heavy in Patmore's blackjack room, heavy with smoke and gin-laden breath, heavy with low talk, suppressed laughter, stifled charges and recriminations, heavy with the suspense of undecided issues in the game.

The deal had fallen to Patmore himself, a large, powerful man with a broad hard face, a bright display of gold teeth, and the complexion of a guinea hen's egg Patmore loved nothing better than to deal blackjack, that swift card game in which each player vied with the dealer to come nearer the coveted value of twenty-one. He loved to taunt the players as he dealt:

'How much you bettin', Saddle-Nose? Six bits and a nickel? Save that nickel for subway fare home—All right, Red Tie, name it. Fifty cents? Don't strain y'self.—Put y' dollar on the table, Clutchin' Hand: 'twon' grow while you squeezin' it.—Next—two bucks to the gen'man with bad hair. Fixin' to get straightened out, ain't you, Kinky?—What you say, Handsome? Two bits? Huh! You ain't so handsome.'

So on about the large round table, covered with the inevitable army blanket. Pat dealt one card to each of the dozen players, noting each bet and adding some uncomplimentary comment. He dealt to himself last. Then he gave a second card to every player, repeating aloud the amounts of their bets. His own two cards he now picked up, held them close to the pearl stick-pin in his lavender tie, and read their value with a pleased smile.

'Gentlemen, I'm hittin',' said he, indicating that since he had not dealt himself a blackjack, the highest possible hand, the players might now draw cards to improve the value of those they already held.

'How 'bout it, Saddle?'

'Hit me,' said that player.

'Remember the number,' warned Patmore. 'Twenty-one, you know. I got a ten-spot here for you. With that fifteen you got, it'll bust you wide open.'

But the player was not to be scared off the draw by the danger of exceeding twenty-one, an eventuality in case of which his bet would be lost.

'If you can read the cards through the back, you can win anyhow,' he said. 'So hit it.'

Pat dealt him a card face-up, a six-spot.

'Thought you said 'twas a ten?' grinned Saddle-Nose. 'Now how much is fifteen and six?'

'It better be fifteen and six,' Pat said, going on to the next player. 'Have one, Liver-Lip?'

'A small one,' requested the so-called Liver-Lip.

'Bing! Ten-spot. Too many? My sympathy. Throw it from you—Next?'

He continued his dealing and his banter, 'busting out' two or three players and finally coming to himself. He now turned up the two cards he already had, revealing a seven and a four.

'Eleven to hit, you shines,' he taunted. 'Every face-card is

a ten in this man's game. Which means the deck is full o'
tens and'—he drew the top card—'I get one of 'em!'
Vehemently he slapped down a king. 'Twenty-one, boogies.
Read 'em and wail.'

None of the remaining hands exceeded a value of twenty,
and Patmore lustily collected from them all. 'Gettin' off tonight,
boys. Smoke this bank over—fifty bucks if it's a nickel—I'm
dealin'. State yo' hopes.'

'I hope,' said Jinx Jenkins, elbowing into line at Pat's immediate right, 'you deal me every lousy dime you get.'

Pat paused. 'It's the freckle-faced giraffe,' observed he, grinning goldenly. 'Where you been, long-gone, doin' time?'

'Been off studyin' black magic.' He put down a dollar. 'Now
I'm go'n' show you how it works.'

But when the round had been played he had lost his dollar

'Add y'self up again, Zero,' advised Pat. 'You got the wrong
answer that time.'

A second dollar Jinx bet. It too joined the pile in front of
the dealer. Said the latter:

'What you need is another dimension, Spring-Board. You
long enough, but you too flat.'

'I admit,' Jinx said, 'I ain't thick as you is. Deal the cards.'

'Ain't reducin', is you?' inquired Pat sarcastically when he
came around to Jinx the third time, noting the latter had put
down only a half-dollar.'

'I'll increase it in a minute—to yo' sorrow,' promised Jinx.

Truly enough, this time he won, and, after the habit of
seasoned players, settled on a campaign of parlaying. His dollar
became two, the two four, the four eight.

'Deal the eight,' he coolly told Patmore.

'You can't win,' Patmore warned him.

'I can't lose, way you dealin'.'

Patmore complied, read his own cards, and smiled. 'It's upon
you, Slew-Foot,' he told Jinx as he dealt the draw to the other
players, for nothing but twenty-one or a blackjack could beat

the pair of tens he himself held. It pleased him further to note that Jinx was scowling murderously now.

'Better get y'self plenty,' he said when he reached his chief opponent. 'You'll need the deck to win.'

Jinx turned up an ace and a jack, the supreme combination, and inquired quite seriously, 'You mean them two ain't enough? I thought this was a blackjack game.'

'Yo' deal,' growled Pat, surrendering the deck and glumly adjusting his accounts with the line. 'Now you think you so good—deal me yo' sixteen bucks.'

'Oh, Mr Patmore,' Jinx protested, shuffling the cards with care, 'you wouldn' take a po' boy's money 'way from him, would you?'

'Deal or pass!' said Patmore grimly, confident in the knowledge that his money was 'long' and that by continuing to 'stop the bank' he must sooner or later win out on a single superior hand.

He cut the pack. Jinx dealt, picked up his own cards and frowned. 'I'm hittin'.'

'Hit yo'self,' advised Pat. 'I got plenty.'

'Do I have to hit these?' asked Jinx, feigning ignorance, as he turned up a king and a queen.

Pat paid him, ominously silent, without even revealing his own hand. The surrounding observers grinned.

'Black magic,' commented somebody.

'Deal the thirty-two,' ordered Pat.

'Must'n' be so inhospitable, Mr Patmore,' Jinx suggested slowly. 'These gen'men here might want to play too, y' understand.'

'Deal it!' snapped Pat.

'Now what kind o' manners is them?' said Jinx, dealing. He picked up his hand. 'Still hittin', Brother Patmore?'

'Hit it.'

Jinx obeyed, dealing a ten-spot face-up.

'That waits,' Brother Patmore grinned.

Jinx turned over his own hand, a six and a five. 'That

don't,' he remarked. 'Now, lemme see. Them two ten-spots was right together befo'. Maybe they is yet.' He hit himself. 'They is,' he scowled in pretended disgust. 'Who the hotel shuffled this deck?'

Pat pushed away his cards with suppressed fury, and as furiously paid his bet with the rest of the cash before him. But Jinx, instead of burying Pat's cards, turned them over for all to see. 'If these gen'men can't play,' said he reproachfully, 'leas' you can do is let 'em look.' Pat had held twenty when Jinx hit twenty-one.

'Lucky boogy, that Patmo',' commented Saddle-Nose.

'Yes,' agreed Liver-Lip. 'Still got his brass teeth.'

'And now, Rev'm Patmore?' Jinx inquired.

'Where you get that Rev'm stuff?' said Patmore, reaching into his pocket.

''Cause you so good to me.'

'Deal the sixty-four,' commanded Patmore, peeling the amount from the roll of bills he habitually carried.

'It's sinful to gamble, Rev'm.'

'Rev'm go'n' preach yo' funeral in a minute,' promised Pat, ascertaining that he held two face-cards, against which only twenty-one or a blackjack could prevail.

Slowly Jinx picked up his two cards, on which rested the fate not only of himself but of his urgently needy friend, Bubber. 'You mean, Rev'm Patmore, I'm uh—daid?' he asked.

'Any son of a buzzard what thinks he can hit four times in a row can't live.'

Unsmilingly Jinx put down his two cards face-up, the ace and jack of spades. 'O death,' he whispered softly, 'where is thy sting?'

'Great head o' the church!' ejaculated Liver-Lip.

'Wonder if the Rev'm 'll play the one-twenty-eight?' speculated Saddle Nose, just audibly enough to be provoking.

Patmore had become terribly calm. 'A grand and twenty-eight if necessary,' he said. 'It's yo' last deal, Dumb-Luck.

One twenty-eight.' He counted it off and put it down under the stares of bulging eyes. 'Deal that little mess.'

Jinx was shuffling absent-mindedly. 'A little while back, Rev'm,' he ruminated, 'you cast aspersions on my 'rithmetic. Remember?'

Pat was silent.

'Seem like you said I couldn' add or sump'm. Well, I ain't much at subtractin' either. Tell me, please suh, how much is fifty cents from a hundred and twenty-eight bucklets?'

'You ain't funny, 'cep'n to look at. Deal.'

'When I started, what you said was 'deal or pass.

Realization of Jinx's intention raised Patmore's blood pressure almost fatally. 'Why, you son of a bow-legged baboon! You mean after runnin' a half a dollar up to—'

Jinx raised a smoothing hand. 'No need fo' us to fuss, good friends as we is, Rev'm. I pass.' He placed the deck in front of the speechless Pat. 'I ain't no hog. Give these other gen'men sump'm to remember you by, too.'

When Pat recovered the use of his limbs, he passed the deck to the next player and called Stud Samson, who had witnessed the whole affair, into a corner of the room.

'You seen that crook?'

'Black magic,' grinned Stud.

'He couldn't have no such luck. He was dealin' zig-zag.'

'Maybe. Anyhow, you hadn' ought to let nobody take that much out the game.'

'Most of it wasn' in the game. Most of it was mine.'

'What you go'n' do 'bout it?'

'I ain't lettin' no crook pull a deal like that.'

'Yes. But talkin' won't un-crook it. What you go'n' do?'

'Nothin'. But you go'n' do plenty.'

'O.K. by me. But I wish it was his boy, Bubber.'

'What I'm thinkin' 'bout won' do Bubber no good, neither.'

'Pull out the cork.'

'Get a couple o' the boys and bring that currency back.'

'He's pretty good with his hands.'

'Bring it back, see?'

'I ain't blind.' Stud Samson grinned and hurried from the room.

Bubber Brown stood staring at the words 'Undertaker and Embalmer'. His eyes fixed on those baleful letters, he absently thrust his hands into his pockets and strode away past the establishment of Martin Dade; then turned, inadvertently bumping into gay promenaders, and strode a like distance in the opposite direction; finally returned to this first position and remained for a time quite still. Presently into his dark reflections shot a ray of hope:

'Maybe the job's already took.'

So saying, he gathered himself together and resolutely approached the entrance.

Despite the warmth of the summer night, he found the inside of the place as cool as a tomb. It was also disturbingly still; even the robust noises of Seventh Avenue—motors, horns, laughing crowds—seemed far away and of another world, as if they had died and left only their pale ghosts to enter here.

'Wonder is I faded like them sounds—?'

He removed his cap and cleared his throat to announce his presence. No one answered, no one appeared. A company of curiously inanimate green things surrounded him—palms, century plants, cacti—and a strange heavy fragrance hung on the air. Black leather chairs sat expectantly about, a black walnut desk backed against one wall, and a tall thin grandfather clock occupied a nearby corner. The clock's hands pointed to eleven-thirty, but the bright brass pendulum was quite motionless.

'Even the clock done passed out,' Bubber observed, whereupon, as if it had heard, the clock contradictorily tolled a sudden solemn note. It startled out of Bubber an exclamatory, 'What kind o' clock is you?'

'Electric,' answered a soft voice behind him.

He whirled to confront a figure which did nothing to restore his lost composure, the tallest, gauntest, blackest man he had ever beheld, a shadow-like creature with hunched angular shoulders and sunken chest, whose long black Prince Albert hung loosely from his body as from a coat rack. He seemed to have appeared out of nowhere, and Bubber felt that if he should reach out to grasp him there would be nothing to grasp.

He stammered, 'Is you—is you—?'

'I'm Dade.'

'Dade—?' whispered Bubber backing off. 'Sho' 'nough?'

'Yes. Yes indeed. Martin Dade. This is my place.'

'Oh.'

'I hope you haven't suffered a loss?' breathed Martin Dade in a soft, low, toneless voice. 'These are bad times for unexpected—ah—losses.'

'They sho' is,' Bubber agreed.

'What loss, may I inquire?'

'My job,' said Bubber simply.

The undertaker's upper lids lifted, revealing the sudden whites of his deepset eyes, then sank to their habitual droop. 'Yo' job,' he repeated slowly. 'Yes. I see. Yo' job.'

Bubber proffered his slip of paper. 'This man recommended me here. But I reckon you got somebody by now.'

'No.'

'You ain't?'

'No 'ndeed.' Martin Dade studied the slip of paper, then raised his eyes to absorb the new applicant. Bubber tried to return the stare, shifting his round weight from foot to foot, and restlessly fingering his cap; but, honest though his effort was, his eyes just refused to go through with it, fell in spite of him, and sought floor, walls and ceiling.

'Where'd you work befo'?'

'Movin' pianos for Isaacs and Company. When Isaacs took low, the job went places.'

'Yes. I buried old man Isaacs. Where you live?

'Mis' Susan Gassoway's, One Twenty-One West a Hundred Forty-Six' Street—'

'Yes. Yes. I know Sister Gassoway well. Yes. I took care o' Brother Gassoway's remains five years ago. Made a ve'y beautiful corpse. Ve'y beautiful. I'll jes' call Sister Gassoway on the 'phone. One moment—'

Weakly Bubber murmured, 'Beautiful corpse!'

Martin Dade had no trouble reaching Sister Susan Gassoway, and from the way in which he surveyed Bubber as he listened with verifying nods, Sister Gassoway was leaving no doubt about the characteristics of her roomer.

'Wal,' the embalmer said, hanging up, 'it's you and you need a job.'

'It was me when I come in,' admitted Bubber.

'I'm go'n' try you. You will be 'sponsible for the appearance of the premises. You get—ah—eighteen dollars a week and a chance to learn the business.'

'Learn which?'

'Embalmin'. You will assis' me in the preparation of all remains.'

'All remains—' Bubber repeated.

'I take it you are at present ignorant of such matters?'

'Yes suh, and ignorance sho' is bliss.'

'You will soon lose yo' disclination. This is the oldest profession on earth.'

'Reckon I mus' have young ideas.'

'The dead is very beautiful. And entirely harmless.'

'Long as they remains remains. But the fust one changes his mind, I'm go'n' choke him with heel-dust.'

'Do you realize,' Martin Dade said, 'what one case means to you—pussonally?'

'Not yet I don't—no suh.'

'One case alone means at leas' a month's wages.'

'Sound like the wages o' sin, don' it?'

'One case—one month's wages. So whenever you here alone, hold ev'ything till I can get to it.'

'You ain't goin' no place, is you?'

'At night you'll be here alone. Lots comes in at night.'

'Yes suh.'

'Now I'm goin' upstairs a moment. You ring my 'partment bell if any my drivers bring in a case.'

Bubber silently wondered, 'Is the man still talkin' 'bout remains or is he switched to liquor?'

'Little after midnight I'll be down and show you 'bout closin' up.'

Bubber's employer glided out of the front door and left him again alone. For a moment his absence was a relief.

'That ain't no natural man,' he muttered. 'Bet he can't cast a shadder. Act like a ghost, only ghos'es is s'posed to be white.'

A door leading into a rear room caught his attention. Inquisitively he approached and opened it, peering into the darkness beyond. Feeling along the inner frame, he found and pressed a switch. A dim ceiling light disclosed a square, bare room in which the strange sweetish odour he had noticed seemed to originate. Against opposite lateral walls stretched two long narrow tables, each covered with a smooth white sheet. On a wall-shelf at his shoulder sat half a dozen large mysterious dark bottles. Otherwise the room was starkly unadorned.

'What a job,' sighed Bubber, closing the door but leaving the light on. He went to the desk and sat down. The tall spectral clock said quarter to twelve.

'Electric,' muttered Bubber.

But nothing happened.

'Wonder what ole Shades-o'-Night went after?'

Still nothing happened. And, after all, this was a cool spot in the midst of Harlem's best and a job in the midst of general idleness. Ere long, stillness became tranquility; a suffusing peace descended upon Bubber. He settled back in the black-leather desk chair, sighed, grinned a broad toothless grin, and indulged in drowsy conjecture:

'Wonder what I'd do sho' 'nough, alone with a remain?'

* * *

One hand caressing many bills in a bulging trouser-pocket, Jinx Jenkins came out and surveyed Patmore's Pool Rooms for Bubber. He moved between the tables toward the street door.

'Any you thugs seen Bubber Brown?'

'Who you mean—Blondie?'

'Couldn' see him if he was here.'

'He done caught air.'

'Which a way he go?'

'Straight through the front door, Sherlock.'

Beyond that no one knew, and Jinx, condemning his friend for an idiot and a deserter, wandered forth into the night. He too set his course westward, intent on viewing the bright lights of Seventh Avenue with the eyes of a successful man. Bubber would inevitably reappear. Meanwhile Jinx had expenditures to contemplate.

At a lank and leisurely gait he turned up Lenox Avenue; halted before a resplendent shop window where a shining display of shoes was offered at three-eighty per pair, positively none higher; moved on toward a still open haberdashery, exhibiting gorgeous orange and purple neckties at forty-eight cents, fancy socks at three pairs for a dollar, green, blue, and tan shirts at eighty-eight cents, and wide-striped undergarments at thirty-nine cents per undergarment; turned to scowl appreciatively at a pretty girl in white and scarlet pyjamas; finally found himself at the corner of One Hundred Thirty-Fourth Street, through which, a crosstown block westward, beckoned magnetic Seventh Avenue.

Jinx knew that this was that ominous block where fights started at any hour of day or night on no apparent provocation, and where somehow people intercepted bullets and blades of steel oftener than on any other street in Harlem. This street was 'bad': it was dark, and it offered quick escape from pursuit. It was the southern boundary of a rectangle whose other borders were the two avenues on the east and west respectively and broad One Hundred Thirty-Fifth Street on the north. The buildings that faced outward on this rectangle all backed on to a common court, and once an offender got into this court, his capture became a remote possibility, since he might now elude his followers by entering some shop or dwelling from the rear.

Ordinarily Jinx, despite his admitted skill in combat, would have avoided One Hundred Thirty-Fourth Street with the same perversity that made him scowl where others grinned. With nothing to lose there was no jest in danger. But tonight, because he had plenty, his contrariness expressed itself in a deliberate decision to stroll through this jungle pathway and challenge fate.

The leisurely pace which he had set had given ample time for Stud Samson and three of his worthiest associates to come within striking distance. Now nothing could have pleased them more than for Jinx to turn through this street. That was perfect.

'Never did like that chinch nohow,' said one of Samson's coworkers. 'Always actin' mad—I git tired o' that foolishness.'

'Tryin' to look bad,' explained another. 'He ain't bad—he jes' bad-lookin'.'

'Cut it—' warned Stud. 'Now listen—'

A short way within the black block, Jinx found himself between two men he did not know.

'Is you Jinx Jenkins?' one asked.

'Who's curious?' Jinx returned.

'Stop and look behind you,' said the other.

'Bad luck,' Jinx demurred.

'Worse not to,' said Samson's voice behind. 'This rod don' bang—it jes' clicks.'

Jinx detracted attention from the fact that he was slyly increasing the pace by saying:

'S'posin' you got the wrong guy?'

'They ain't but one like you.'

'S'posin',' Jinx insisted, walking quite rapidly now, 'you miss the fust shot?'

'At this distance—' began Stud but never finished; for suddenly Jinx dropped into a low crouch and whirled about, his shoulder catching Samson against the knees. He straightened up, sending the astonished Stud sprawling and in the same movement brought up a fist against the chin of Samson's partner. Seeing himself outnumbered, however, he sidestepped the charge of the remaining two, managed to tread on the momentarily floored Samson's chest, and broke for the open entrance of the nearest apartment house.

Unfortunately his assailants were as familiar with the possibilities of the court as he. They waited only till Stud regained his feet and all plunged in after him.

At the rear end of the hallway Jinx found a window which opened on to the court. Through it he scrambled and yanked down the sash, but had not travelled ten yards through the darkness before he heard it yanked back up with equal vehemence.

'Wonder is that fool got a gun sho' 'nough?'

As swiftly as possible he travelled toward Seventh Avenue, keeping in the dense shadow close to the buildings, avoiding collisions with barrels, boxes, trash-cans, aware that his pursuers were but a few yards behind him and knew where he was though they could not see him. Something overhead knocked off his hat and he dared not stop to retrieve it.

As he approached the Seventh Avenue row of rear-ends, the urgency of his predicament increased. Several ground-floor windows, representing the backs of shops still open, were lighted. To pass one of these might reveal him definitely to his enemies, and to enter one might call for some elaborate and delaying explanation to satisfy the shopkeeper. Discovery of a pocket full of loose bills would not improve his position in case of such trouble.

The first lighted window in the row was very dim but not dim enough, and already he was so near it that he could see inside. That half of the room which he could see was untenanted. Against one bare wall stretched a long narrow table draped with a smooth white sheet.

'Oh-oh,' he grunted. 'A gun behind me and a morgue in front. Mistuh Lindbergh, where is you now?'

But as he came to the corner near the window, he collided with an idea. 'Judas Priest!' he said softly. 'That's brains!'

He listened intently. The others were nearing slowly, surely, apparently investigating every darker recess they passed. Jinx's uncertainty vanished. He sidled along the wall to the open, dim-lighted window, he extended one long leg along the sill and without exposing his body, got that leg inside; then swift as a shadow, slipped his body in and drew the other leg after, not having obliterated more than a quarter of the window's light at any moment. Still he might have been seen; and so once inside he lost no time; tiptoed to the nearer table, turned back the sheet, stretched his length supine on the hard narrow surface, and, without compunction, pulled the sheet up over his head.

'Might as well be dead as get killed,' he growled and lay still.

Something roused Bubber out of his doze. He blinked, looked about, and with an abrupt chill realized his whereabouts. At the same time he became certain that he had not just waked— that something had waked him. And with all his original misgivings, his attention focused on the door to the rear room.

It was an unusually wide and heavy door having a flat, smooth mahogany surface, unbroken even by panelling.

'Look like it's hidin' sump'm,' Bubber observed. Then he gave a snort of disgust and turned his back to prove he wasn't afraid. 'Shuh, I done looked in there.'

The door however remained the centre of his universe, and he suddenly spun around to look again, much as if he expected to catch it by surprise. But it was not to be caught off guard, betrayed not the slightest inclination to swing slowly wide and reveal some spectral horror beyond its threshold, remained stolidly, squarely, blankly shut, expressionless as a mask. Its very impassiveness suggested concealment. Against his will his eyes fixed themselves on it, and it soullessly gave back his stare.

'Jes' like a glass eye.'

Presently the struggle against the pull of that concealment lifted him out of his chair and set him to pacing back and forth across the room. He thrust his hands into his pockets and whistled. That didn't help; the sound faded out a few inches from the lips like the vapour of breath on cold air.

'Only thing to do,' he decided, when at last he could endure the distress no longer, 'is look ag'in.'

Slowly he started toward that door, moving with great caution, as if he feared his approach might be overheard. With one hand on the knob, he stopped and turned his head sideways to listen. Hearing nothing, he carefully pulled the door a little way open and thrust his head a little way in.

For one paralysed instant something like an electric shock grasped his rotund figure, squeezed it into a knot, then released it. He wheeled, the heavy door, automatically restrained, sighed too, too slowly shut, and Bubber, still clutching the knob, leaned limply back against it, his face a sight to behold.

'Is I dreamin',' he whispered, 'or is I dreamin'?'

After a moment the sheer incredibility of it overwhelmed his consternation. He turned back and fearsomely cracked the door to look again. With so small an aperture, he could make out only the more distant table, which was still unoccupied. He pulled the door wider, and sure enough there it was: on the nearer table lay a long, unquestionably human form, covered from head to foot by a smooth white sheet.

'Sump'm tells me,' Bubber thought, 'I ain't go'n' be here long.' Then he remembered. 'But I got to stay. Yonder lay my fust month's wages. Lemme go call the man.'

But ere he could drag his eyes from that shocking miracle, something began to happen, something as monstrously awful as to turn even Bubber ashen. The figure on the table began to move.

At first the movement was stealthy, as if this creature too apprehended discovery. Then slowly, inch by inch, the head began to rise, and a rippling movement beside the trunk indicated that one of the hands was coming up to uncover the rising head.

It did not succeed. With an alacrity born of terror, Bubber seized one of the bottles on the shelf at his shoulder and brought it down with a thud on the shrouded skull.

'Dead you is and dead you remains,' he vowed, as the figure fell back into place.

With the bottle still in hand he swung about and breathlessly started for the street door. Ere he reached it, the black form and white eyes of Martin Dade loomed into the entrance like the shadow of death. Bubber stopped, mumbling, 'What a place—the dead livin' and the livin' dead.'

Martin Dade pointed to the bottle. 'Whass that?' he breathed.

Bubber held it up as though he hadn't seen it before.

'Embalmin' fluid,' identified the undertaker, sepulchrally.

'No?' said Bubber.

'What you doin' with it?'

'Uh—tryin' it out. Come 'eh. Look in yonder.'

Dade glided forward, opened the rear room door, and entered, followed by a gingerly Bubber. The undertaker showed no surprise. 'Yas—that case I was expectin'. Yas. Less get right to work.'

'But—but listen—,' began Bubber.

'No time fo' buttin' now,' Martin Dade said and pulled down the upper end of the sheet. And even if Bubber had been permitted to go on, he would have halted now, recognizing the familiar yellow, freckled countenance of his friend and ally, Jinx.

His mouth opened and shut. He swallowed and stared. Finally he managed a curious whisper:

'My—fust—month's—wages—'

If the undertaker could have seen Bubber's face at that moment, even he would have stopped to investigate. But the half-pint of nightcap which he had gone upstairs to consume as his regular evening rite had combined now with professional enthusiasm to blind him to everything but the work at hand.

Deftly he unbuttoned Jinx's soft shirt. While Bubber looked on with greater impotence than that of fright, the embalmer procured instruments.

Bubber stood behind him, staring at Jinx's face, hearing not a word of Dade's instructions.

'Fust thing to do—'

Then suddenly he realized Dade's intention. 'Hol' on!' burst from him. 'Listen, mistuh—'

'Nothing' to be scairt of,' Martin Dade reassured him, not bothering to turn at the cry. 'All you got to do—'

In the moment's desperation Bubber needed no one to tell him what to do. He saw but one thing to do and he was on the point of doing it. The bottle, which he had not relinquished, came up over Dade's unaware head.

'What it takes to embalm with, I got—' he said, and would have neutralized his first blow with a second. But it was unnecessary.

It was unnecessary because Jinx was the perverse fellow he was and behaved accordingly. Anyone else would have remained stunned too long; or hearing Bubber's familiar voice and coming to normally, would have slowly opened his eyes and inquired, 'Where am I?' But being Jinx, he did none of these things; instead, he sat suddenly bolt upright and growled wrathfully.

'What the hell—?'

'Wah—!' said Martin Dade, backing off and dropping his instruments. Jinx, not fully conscious but exceedingly active, got off the table and, with the sheet still clinging to him, approached the embalmer scowling. The embalmer gave up and closed his eyes, went limp and crumpled to the floor.

But Bubber's face had broken into a broad grin of joyous relief. 'Hot dam! Go to it, Lazarus!'

Jinx scrambled out of the sheet and recognized Bubber. 'What the hell—?' he repeated balefully.

'What the hell, yo'self,' said Bubber.

The sight of the bottle in Bubber's hand jogged Jinx's memory. He rubbed his head. 'Did you hit me with that?'

Bubber was reproachful. 'You know no glass bottle could hit yo' haid and stay whole. Look. 'Tain't even cracked.'

'Well, what hit me, then?'

'Nemmine that. What I want to know is what you doin' daid?'

The question quite cleared Jinx's foggy senses. He thrust his hand into his pocket and withdrew bills, grunting with satisfaction to find that he still had them.

'Reckon,' Bubber observed, 'with that much money I'd passed out, too. Come on—less get out this place befo' sump'm else happen what can't.'

When Dade awoke he found the bottle of embalming fluid nestling in the crook of his arm. And on making his bewildered way from the floor of the rear room to the office in front, he discovered a pencilled note stuck in a panel of the electric clock:

I resigns.
  Bubber Brown.
  P.S. You don't owe me nothing. I took a month's wages with me.

AN INTRODUCTION TO CONTEMPORARY HARLEMESE

Expurgated and Abridged

AIN'T GOT 'EM
Possesses no virtues—is no good.

ASK FOR
Challenge to battle in terms that don't mean maybe.

BELLY-RUB
An indelicate but accurate designation of any sexy dance, the *bump* being the popular current example.

BIGGY
Sarcastic abbreviation of 'big boy'.

BOOGY
Negro. A contraction of *Booker T.*, used only of and by members of the race. My own favourite among all the synonyms of Negro, of which the following are current: *Cloud, crow, darkey, dinge, dinky, eight-ball, hunk, hunky, ink, jap, jasper, jig, jigaboo, jigwalker, joker, kack, Mose, race-man, race-woman, Sam, shade, shine, smoke, spade, aigaboo.*

BOY
Friend and ally. Buddy.

BRING MUD
To fall below expectations, disappoint. He who escorts a homely *sheba* to a *dicky shout* brings mud.

BROTHER
A form of address, usually ironic. A bystander, witnessing the arrest of some offender, may observe: 'It's too bad now, brother.'

BUMP; BUMPTY-BUMP;
  BUMP-THE-BUMP
A *shout* characterized by a forward and backward swaying of the hips. Said to be an excellent aphrodisiac. Also said to be the despair of *fays*.

BUTT
Buttocks.

CAN
Buttocks.

CATCH AIR
To take leave, usually under urgent pressure.

CHOKE
To defeat. To *turn one's damper down*.

CHORINE
A chorus girl.

CHORAT
A chorus man.

CLOUD
See *boogy*.

CROW
See *boogy*.

DADDY
Provider of affection and other more tangible delights.

DARKEY
See *boogy*.

DICKTY
Adj.—Swell.
Noun—High-toned person.

DINGE
See *boogy*.

DINKY
See *boogy*.

DOG
Any extraordinary person, thing, or event 'Ain't this a dog?' is a comment on anything unusual.

DO IT!; DO THAT THING!; DO YOUR STUFF!
'More power to ye!'

DOWN THE WAY
Designation of some place familiar to both parties talking.

DO ONE'S STUFF
Exhibit one's best. Show off.

EIGHT-BALL
A dark-skinned black man or woman. (The number 8 pool ball is black.)

EVERMORE
Extremely, as in 'evermore red-hot mamma'.

DRUNK DOWN
Plumbing the nadir of inebriation. Soused to helplessness.

FAY; OFAY
A person who, so far as is known, is white. *Fay* is said to

be the original term and *ofay* a contraction of 'old' and 'fay'.

FREEBY
Something for nothing, as complimentary tickets to a theatre.

FROM WAY BACK
Of extraordinary experience and skill.

GET AWAY
As in get away with something. Escape unpunished for audacity and to triumph, as does the successful *jiver* or the winner at blackjack.

GIVE ONE AIR
To dismiss one with finality. To 'give one the gate'.

GRAVY
Unearned increment. *Freeby*.

GREAT DAY IN THE MORNING!
Exclamation of wonder.

HAUL IT
Haul *hiney*. Depart in great haste. *Catch air*. *It*, without an obvious antecedent, usually has pelvic significance. 'Put *it* in the chair' means 'Sit down'.

HIGH
Enjoying the elevated spirits of moderately advanced inebriation. *Tight* in the usual slang sense. Cf. *tight* in the Harlemese sense.

HINEY
Affectionate diminutive for hind-quarters. 'It's your hiney' means 'It will cost you your hiney', i. e. 'You are undone'.

HOT
Kindling admiration. As 'overdone' among *jigs* as is 'marvellous' among *fays*.

HOT YOU!
Pronounced 'hot-choo'. Equivalent to *Oh, no, now!*

HOW COME?
Why?

HUNK; HUNKY
See *boogy*.

I MEAN
'You said it.' Ex 'Some *sheba*, huh?'—'I *mean*.'

INK
See *boogy*.

JAP
See *boogy*.

JASPER
See *boogy*.

JAZZ
1. The modern American musical idiom, of course.
2. Sometimes synonymous with *jive*.

JIG; JIGABOO; JIGWALKER
See *boogy*.

JIVE
1. Pursuit in love or any device thereof. Usually flattery with intent to win.
2. Capture.
In either sense this word implies passing fancy, hence deceit.

JIVER
One who *jives*.

JOHN-BROWN
'Doggone.'

JOKER
See *boogy*.

KACK
Extreme sarcasm for *dickty*.

K.M.
Kitchen mechanic, i.e., cook, girl, scullion, menial.

LONG-GONE
Lost. State in which 'it's one's *hiney*'.

LORD TODAY!
Exclamation of wonder.

MAMMA
Potential or actual sweetheart.

MARTIN
Jocose designation of death. Derived from Bert Williams' story: *Wait Till Martin Comes*.

MISS
Fail. A question is characteristically answered by use of *miss* or some equivalent expression. 'Did you win money?'—'I didn't miss' or 'Do you mean me?'—'I don't mean your brother' and so on.

MONKEY-BACK
Dude.

MONKEY-MAN
'Cake-eater'.

MOSE
See *boogy*.

MISS ANNE; MR CHARLIE
Non-specific designation of 'swell' whites. 'Boy, boot-legging pays. That boogy's got a straight-eight just like *Mr Charlie's*.'—'Yea, and his *mamma*'s got a fur coat just like *Miss Anne's*, too.'

MUD
See *bring mud*.

NO LIE
You said it. *I mean*.

OFAY
See *fay*.

OH, NO, NOW!
Exclamation of admiration.

OSCAR
Dumb-bell.

OUT (OF) THIS WORLD
Beyond mortal experience or belief.

PAPA
1. See *daddy*
2. Equivalent to *brother*.

PLAY THAT
'Play that game', hence to countenance or tolerate.

POKE OUT
Be distinguished, excel.

PREVIOUS
Premature, hence, presumptuous. He who tries to break into a ticket-line is likely to be warned, 'Don't get too *previous, brother*.'

PUT ONE IN
To report one to some enemy or authority in order to have one punished.

PUT (GET, HAVE) THE LOCKS ON
To handcuff. Hence to render helpless. Most frequently heard in reference to some form of gambling, such as card games and love affairs.

PUT IT ON ONE
To injure one deliberately.

RACE-MAN (WOMAN)
See *boogy*

RED-HOT
Somewhat hotter than *hot*. Extremely striking.

RIGHT
Somewhat in excess of perfection.

RIGHT ON
Nevertheless.

RAT
Antithesis of *dickty*

SALTY DOG
Stronger than *dog*.

SAM
See *boogy*

SEE ONE GO
Give one aid. '*See me go* for breakfast?' means 'Pay for my breakfast?' It is the answerer's privilege to interpret the query literally, thus: 'See you go—to hell.'

SHARP
Striking 'keen'. A beautifully dressed woman is '*sharp out this world*'.

SHEBA
Queen. Frail. Broad.

SHOUT
1. Ball. Prom.
2. A slow one-step in which all the company gets happy.

SLIP
1. To kid.
2. *To slip in the dozens*, to disparage one's family.

SMOKE
See *boogy*.

SMOKE OVER
To give the once over. Observe critically.

SMOOTHE
Verb—To calm, to quell anger. What *sweet mamma* does to *cruel papa* when he gets *tight*.
Adj.—1. Cunning, 'slick as a *smoothe jiver*'. 2.—Faultless.

STRUT ONE'S STUFF
See *do one's stuff*.

STUFF
1. Talent, as above.
2. Hokum. Baloney. Banana
oil. 'They tell me that *sheba*
tried to commit suicide over
her *daddy*.'—'Huh. That's a
lot of stuff.'

TELL 'EM!; TELL 'EM
  'BOUT IT!
Exclamation of agreement
and approval.

THE MAN
Designation of abstract
authority. He who trespasses
where a sign forbids is
asked: 'Say, *biggy*, can't you
read *the man's sign*?'

THERE AIN'T NOTHING
  TO THAT
This signifies complete
agreement with a previous
assertion. It is equivalent to
saying, 'That is beyond question.'

TIGHT
Tough. Redoubtable. Hard.
Not 'drunk' in the usual
sense, for which the
Harlemese is *high*.

TO BE HAD
To be bested.

TO BE ON
To bear actual or pretended
malice against.

TOO BAD
1. Marvellous.
2. Extremely unfortunate.

TOOTIN'
Right. Unquestionable. Full
remark is 'You are doggone
tootin'.'

TURN THEM ON
Strut one's stuff.

TURN ONE'S DAMPER
  DOWN
To reduce the temperature of
one who is *hot*, hence to
choke.

UH-HUH
Yes.

UH-UH
No.

UPPITY
High-hat.

WHAT DO YOU SAY?
How do you do?

CAN'T SAY IT
No complaint.

ZIGABOO
See *boogy*.

Also available

The Conjure-Man Dies

Rudolph Fisher

'Highly readable, wholly entertaining'   STANLEY ELLIN

When the body of N'Gana Frimbo, the African conjure-man, is dis-covered in his consultation room, Perry Dart, one of Harlem's ten Black police detectives, is called in to investigate. Together with Dr Archer, a physician from across the street, Dart is determined to solve the baffling mystery, helped and hindered by Bubber Brown and Jinx Jenkins, local boys keen to clear themselves of suspicion of murder and undertake their own investigations.

The Conjure-Man Dies was the very first detective novel written by an African-American. A distinguished doctor and accomplished musician and dramatist, Rudolph Fisher was one of the principal writers of the Harlem Renaissance, but died in 1934 aged only 37. With a gripping plot and vividly drawn characters, Fisher's witty novel is a remarkable time capsule of one of the most exciting eras in the history of Black fiction.

This crime classic is introduced by New York crime writer Stanley Ellin, and also includes Rudolph Fisher's last published story, 'John Archer's Nose', in which Perry Dart and Dr Archer return to solve the case of a young man murdered in his own bed.

'A well-constructed thriller of a little-known side of Harlem life, with a black detective to solve the crime and with just enough humour on the side'
                                        NEW YORK TIMES

Also available

Trent's Last Case

E. C. Bentley

A powerful and ruthless American capitalist is found dead in the garden of his English country house. But why is he not wearing his false teeth? And why is his young widow so relieved at his death? Sent by his newspaper to investigate, journalist and amateur detective Philip Trent encounters a lot more than he bargained for.

Written as the result of a wager with Father Brown author G. K. Chesterton, *Trent's Last Case* was Edmund Bentley's attempt to write a novel that would ridicule the stale conventions of detective fiction. Unwittingly, he produced what Agatha Christie called 'one of the best detective stories ever written'. Its flesh-and-blood characters, easy humour and cunning solution became the prototype for an entire generation of crime writers, although few ever matched the genius of *Trent's Last Case*.

This Crime Club classic is introduced by Golden Age fiction expert and writer Dr John Curran, and also includes a unique afterword by Dorothy L. Sayers, who described it as 'the one detective story of the present century which I am certain will go down to posterity as a classic. It is a masterpiece.'

'One of the best detective stories ever written.'

AGATHA CHRISTIE